A FAREWELL KISS

LOCKHART REGENCY ROMANCE

LAURA ROLLINS

ALSO BY LAURA ROLLINS

Lockhart Regency Romance

Courting Miss Penelope—available at LauraRollins.com

Wager for a Lady's Hand

Lily for my Enemy

A Heart in the Balance

A Farewell Kiss

A Well-Kept Promise

A Dickens of a Christmas

The Hope of Christmas Past

The Joy of Christmas Present

The Peace of Christmas Yet to Come

To Mikaela,
The best kindred-spirit a girl could have asked for.

CHAPTER 1

*L*ord Quintin Lockhart pulled his hat further down atop his head and squinted out across the field. Dozens of white specks covered the grey land. For a moment, he imagined them other-worldly spirits, come to haunt the winter field and strike fear into the most stalwart of hearts.

Truly, though, they were just sheep. Martin Soames' sheep. It was a large herd, but not as large as it should have been.

"Bad news, my lord," Martin Soames said, striding up the hill toward Quintin, his heavy breath coming out in small puffs of clouds around his mouth. "We lost another two last night."

Quintin opened and closed a fist repeatedly. If they didn't figure out what was infecting the sheep, and soon, Martin was on track to lose nearly an eighth of the herd before spring. And that *was* enough to strike fear into the most stalwart of hearts. Of all the things Quintin had faced the past several years since taking on this estate, including becoming master over its various farmers, this was his biggest obstacle yet.

"Keep the other sheep away from the carcasses."

"I've ordered them burned, same as before."

"Good plan." But keeping the other sheep away from the

diseased carcasses wasn't proving enough. "I think it's time we try ordering all new feed. We'll toss the old and see if that doesn't make a difference." There was a chance, small though it might be, that the grain was what was making his sheep sick.

"My lord." Martin looked at him with wide eyes. "That'll be mighty expensive. 'Nd I'm already not looking so good in the profits area this year."

"The mathematics will look even worse if you keep losing sheep." In his exasperation, Quintin's hand fell to his side, colliding with his work trousers. A plume of dust billowed out at the impact. "And don't worry about the cost. I'll see to the new feed."

Martin bowed low. "Thank you, my lord." The man's voice was thick with emotion.

"Don't mention it."

Martin nodded, pulling deferentially on his forelock and turned to leave.

Quintin watched him go. Martin was a hard worker and only two years his junior, though it was clear from their many conversations that he not only respected Quintin as his master but trusted his advice. Martin had inherited the dilapidated sheep farm from his father, who'd been far more inclined to drink than herd sheep. In so many ways, Martin and Quintin were alike. Granted, one may have been master and the other farmer, but they both wanted nothing more than to make the bit of land they were responsible for successful.

Still, Martin was right. He'd already paid for the next two months of grain. To toss it all and pay for new feed would be quite a waste if it wasn't the cause of the sheep's plight.

"Martin," Quintin called. The sheep farmer stopped and looked back. "Don't get rid of the old grain. Just set it aside for now; if the new grain doesn't help, that proves the old isn't bad. Hold onto it just in case."

After another pull at his hair, the man moved away once more.

Blast this sheep farm. When Father had first mentioned that this estate—Cottonhold—was not linked to the holdings Quintin's older brother was to inherit, Quintin had thought it the perfect opportunity. He'd moved here immediately after finishing at Cambridge and begun looking over the books and speaking with all the farmers and families under its care.

He could still remember the first time he'd stood here, atop the tallest of the many hills, and looked out over the land. He'd fancied himself something of a brave knight like in those many books Father had read him as a child, here to reclaim the land from a devious monster. He still often felt that way—a truth he carefully hid from all eyes and ears. But reality was, the monster was not only in his mind. Neglect and disease were as devious monsters as had ever laid waste to any land.

Cottonhold had once been aptly named, but when Quintin had first arrived, it was only turning enough of a profit to support itself; not enough to support a gentleman overseeing the estate, nor enough for that gentleman to wed or have a family.

Quintin ran a hand down his face. His only objective these past four years had been to see Cottonhold make a sizable profit once more. And during these past four years, he'd not managed it once. Quintin placed both his hands against his hips and leaned back, stretching. It had been another strenuous day. The muscles along his back ached at the pull. His hands hurt, too.

That was something else that hadn't met his expectations these past years; he'd originally envisioned himself as the man behind the books. The one who met with his man of business often, and, even more often, rode out across the vast land to check on farms and herds and whatnot.

He hadn't envisioned himself spending every day in breeches covered in sheep dung, shirts stained from sweat and dirt, and a large brim hat no different than the one the workers wore. Gads, if anyone were to ride by right now, they'd most assuredly mistake him for a hired hand, not the third son of a marquess. But turning a profit meant more work initially, which required funds he didn't have. The obvious solution was to have everyone take on additional responsibilities; master or no, that included him.

Quintin spun on his heel and headed back toward the house. At least Cottonhold had an excellent cook. He arrived feeling in slightly better spirits than he had that morning. The house smelled of baking bread and something else. Soup, perhaps? That was exactly what he needed after a grueling day of calluses and filthy boots.

He couldn't deny the other thing he'd not expected when he first took on this farm—Quintin enjoyed working with his hands. He didn't mind the dirt, though the smell still got to him now and then. And, though he had a good eye for mathematics and could tally a cost and profits sheet with confidence, nothing left him feeling as fulfilled as discussing the day-to-day issues his farmers struggled with and counseling them on what to do next. Perhaps, if the heavens had seen fit to send him down during the Renaissance instead of now, he would have made a better councilor than knight.

Finally clean—his valet had been disillusioned every bit as quickly as Quintin had when they had first arrived—Quintin sat at the long table, across from his man of business, John Willoughby. Quintin ate alone far more often than not at Cottonhold. Sometimes John joined him, or sometimes neighbors visited. Either way, the solitude was not something that bothered Quintin.

"Any good news today?" John asked, his tone far from hopeful.

Quintin had been right; soup was placed before them first. "No." He picked up his spoon and scooped up a bit of potato and carrot. "We lost two more today."

John was never anything less than professional and wholly proper, but Quintin could still sense the curse hiding just behind the man's tightly closed mouth. They ate in silence for several minutes. What was there to be said? The sheep farm was in deeper trouble than it had ever been in. If they didn't stop this newest blight, who knew what Quintin would be forced to do? Moreover, though the other farms under the watch of Quintin's estate were doing all right, none of them were doing particularly well.

In the silence, Quintin's mind wandered to the one person he never truly stopped thinking about—Lady Esther Collingwood. What was she doing this very moment? Probably sitting down to supper as he was. She'd always complained about the cook her family employed. Always said the woman didn't know a turnip from a tomato. Was the cook still boiling potatoes so long they were not but colorless, flavorless mush? Was she still providing overly sweet tea and overly tart cake when Esther had visitors? He couldn't help but smile as he recalled how she'd gone on and on about such things one holiday when he'd returned from Cambridge for a visit. Truth was, Esther was the reason Quintin spent months interviewing different cooks before hiring the one he now employed. He was determined to make this home everything Esther could want and more, and that would indubitably require an excellent cook.

Esther's entire family had been visiting her Uncle in India these past two years, but they were finally home once more. They'd spoken but briefly during Cassandra and Nigel's wedding. He'd been overjoyed to see her again; at first, he'd thought she felt the same. Only … there had been a bit of hesitancy in her tone when they'd spoken, a bit of withdrawal in the way she had looked at him.

There had been a time when both had believed their connection would be of the everlasting kind. Was she of a different mind now than before? Had India changed her? Or was it simply the influence of time?

Then again, while they'd been free to gallop and gossip all across the countryside as children, society did not allow for such things now that they were both adults. Perhaps he ought to attribute her reserved manner to that.

"Cottonhold is in rather a dire situation, I'll agree with you there."

Quintin let out a long sigh. John, while professional, did have a tendency to profess everything doomed to fail. As of yet, Quintin had not had enough success to prove him otherwise. That was a sobering realization.

"We've tackled difficulties before," Quintin said. "We'll right this one, too."

John didn't seem convinced and ate his meal with nothing even close to a smile.

All Quintin cared about was getting this place ready to accept a wife. He'd had a moment of panic last spring when he'd heard rumors that the Earl of Harrington, Esther's father, had returned with his family for the sole purpose of Esther's coming out. A few quick inquiries had proven the family to be in India a while longer and Quintin had relaxed, believing he had until spring to get his house in order.

Though, now, that only left him two more months. He couldn't imagine that being enough time.

After supper Quintin sat with John and discussed their various options over port. New feed was to be ordered for Martin post haste. Though John was not pleased that Quintin had agreed to pay for the new feed himself, he didn't argue that it was a sound idea.

There was a well-respected sheep doctor two counties north; they agreed to summon the man and see what he could tell them. They discussed moving the herd to a different area at great length. Such would be costly and dangerous since spring was still several weeks away. But if it was that or lose an ever-greater portion of the herd, then Quintin would have to consider it.

A man servant walked in, a letter atop a silver platter. "Pardon me, my lord," the old man said in long, drawn out tones, "but this just arrived."

Quintin's brow creased. He'd already received that morning's post. This letter must have been quite important to be sent by courier. He accepted the letter off the tray and the manservant bowed and left.

Quintin recognized the handwriting immediately. It was from his sister, Cassandra, and was marked from London. Strange; he hadn't known Cassandra was there just now. He'd felt certain she was settling into her new home with her new husband, Lord Nigel Southcott. Now there was a man who would have made an excellent knight. Other than Cassandra, Quintin was the only Lockhart who knew Nigel's true occupation—a special carrier of information from spies to the British aristocracy.

If Quintin failed completely at being master of the estate, perhaps he could ask Nigel for a position. At least then his dreams of heroism and valor would not completely go to waste. Quintin flipped the letter over even as he smirked to himself; he'd always thought his penchant for fairy tales and mystical stories would fade as he grew older. It had for everyone around him. Yet, there was part of him that had never fully let any of them go.

The letter was quite short.

Quintin,

We arrived in London to purchase a few things for Sheldon and Marianne.

Oh, well that made sense. He'd heard that she was in the family way. Quintin was ever so happy for his brother, if a touch jealous of Sheldon for having already secured the hand of the woman he loved.

While at Almack's the other night, we happened across none other than Lady Esther Collingwood.

Quintin stood abruptly. Esther was in London? So early in the year? His hands suddenly felt cold. Lord Harrington had never arrived in Town so early, at least, never before now.

"Lud," John said with a start. "Do not tell me today holds more bad news."

Quintin waved the statement away and continued reading.

It seems she made her bows some weeks ago.

Thought you'd like to know.

Yrs,

Etc.

Esther had made her bows. She was even now attending balls and meeting rows of gentlemen, no doubt. They would be lining up and filling up her dance card. Quintin may have known Esther— loved Esther—when she was only in pigtails and freckles, but he wasn't the least bit blind to the gorgeous woman she'd blossomed in to. Nor was he blind to the fact that many other gentlemen were bound to take notice of her, too.

"I must away," Quintin said, even as he strode toward the door.

"You cannot be serious," John said, standing and following him out. "The estate is in the middle of a most delicate situation."

Quintin crossed to the stairs but paused at the bottom and turned back toward John. "I should be back shortly. Order the new feed and see what the sheep doctor has to say. Keep me informed."

"Please forgive my bluntness, sir, but you simply cannot leave just now."

Not leave? What good was it if the estate turned a larger profit than any in all of England if Esther was not beside him? He'd only taken on the estate as a means of securing a future home for a wife and family. That wife could only ever be one woman—and that woman was currently being courted by who knew how many other men. Quintin felt a crushing weight press down on his shoulders. He'd promised he'd be there when she had her season.

Yet, she had been out for weeks now—weeks!—and what had he been doing? Mucking about in sheep dung and wool.

Quintin shook his head. "You can reach me at my family's house in London." Quintin hurried up the stairs.

"You're going to London?" John apparently had not yet accepted this new turn in events, for he continued to follow. "What could you possibly hope to accomplish there?"

Only the single most important thing Quintin would ever do in his life—openly win the hand of Lady Esther Collingwood.

The memory of her smaller than normal smile from last time they had spoken rose to the surface and a feeling he'd never had before wormed its way into his chest where it sat, painful and sharp.

Would she have him if he courted her?

Did she even still want him?

Quintin shook his head and shoved the uncertain feeling away even as he turned at the landing and faced John. "I am going to London. Is that clear? You are to see to things here."

Quintin was not prone to strict tones or harsh demands, but right now he had the most pressing of businesses weighing on him and he could not care less about Cottonhold and its determination to fail. "I pay you well, John. It's time you prove your worth."

With that, he spun around and marched toward his bed chambers. If only he could borrow Helios' chariot at a time such as this and fly to London as quick as a bird. Quintin shook his head and rung for his valet. He had much to pack and no time to lose.

CHAPTER 2

*L*ady Esther Collingwood sat with her hands most decidedly *not* twisting about each other atop her lap. Would he be here tonight? Her gaze moved over the various couples dancing to a lovely minuet, all of whom were quite unaware of her distress. She only gave the ladies in their flowing gowns, beaded necklaces, and flowery hairdo's a passing glance. But the gentlemen? Well, she scrutinized each and every one who passed her. At least, until she knew for certain he wasn't her Quintin Lockhart, and then she ignored each one as much as she did the ladies.

"What a merry time we are having, are we not?" Esther's mother, Lady Mary Collingwood, Countess of Harrington, said.

Esther nodded. "Yes, quite." Of course, she'd be having a much merrier time if the room wasn't so warm. Or if her lady's maid hadn't tied her corset quite so tight.

Most of all, she felt certain she wouldn't be merry at all this season once her Quintin had arrived. She'd happened across his two sisters some days previous. No doubt they would have informed Quintin that she had come out several weeks earlier than even she had expected. He would come. Quintin had been a perfect gentleman even as a boy, and she'd seen him grow only kinder and more trustworthy as he became a man. She had no doubt in her mind he would come.

Ever since she was a little girl she'd looked forward to this moment. Now it was here, and all she could do was desperately hope that tonight *wouldn't* be the night she saw Quintin again.

For years, they'd been planning this. Ever since they had been children. He'd taken her hand and pulled her beneath the flowing branches of a weeping willow. He'd even kissed her; well, on the cheek anyway. But for two children only eleven and eight, it had felt like a moment from a fairytale. He'd promised he'd never love another, and that she needn't worry when it came time for her to make her bows. He'd be right there beside her.

"Dear me," Mother said, "that was as melancholy a sigh as I've ever heard. Are you quite all right?"

"I am fine," Esther said quickly. She sat up straighter. The chair she was sitting on, while quite obliging and perfectly situated by the back door where there was a small breeze was, nonetheless, excessively hard.

"Don't worry." Mother's voice dropped softer. "I have been busy this week, you know. Speaking with other matrons, paving the path. Give it some time."

Esther only nodded again. If Quintin was in attendance tonight, surely she would have seen him by now. Perhaps she had been granted another night's reprieve. She didn't deserve such mercy.

Whatever would she say to him once they *did* meet? If he ever found out what she'd done, he would think her a cruel coward. She could bear anything if only she could avoid her Quintin finding out the truth.

"Pardon me."

Esther turned toward the voice.

Lord Albert Fawcett, Earl of Copeland stood nearby with a small glass of punch in one hand. The paunchiness of his middle was mostly concealed by a well-tailored jacket and vest, but with him standing over her, Esther could not miss it. "I have brought this for you, my lady"—he held the punch out to Mother then turned to Esther—"and for you, I brought the hope that you might join me for the next set."

"I would be honored." Esther smiled as she took his hand and stood, but she didn't miss Mother's I-told-you-so look.

Lord Copeland led her to the dance floor as other couples flocked to the center of the room, forming two long lines. The loquacious Lady Christina Enfield stood to Esther's left and the slender Miss Rebecca—whose surname Esther had never fully caught—stood to her right.

Across from Miss Rebecca was a man gossiped to be a womanizer. Esther wanted to scowl in his direction. Men like him should not be allowed to attend balls and the like. Did Miss Rebecca know the type she was dancing with? Unbidden, guilt swelled up inside of Esther. She lifted her chin and tried to force the emotion away. She was here to forget about India. Here to forget what she'd done.

Wordless, they flowed into the beginning of the dance. Lord Copeland could not have been called graceful, yet he executed the dance with exactness. While he wasn't as tall as her Quintin and wouldn't have been considered handsome by any of the young ladies in the room, he was still respectable. The heir to a prominent seat in Lords, too. No doubt, Mother was quite pleased that he'd asked her to stand.

He took hold of her hand, his other hand going to the small of her back and they turned slowly around each other, ending where they'd begun the dance only a few minutes before. The movement brought them closer together than society usually allowed. Though not as old as her father, he certainly was advanced in years. It appeared as though his cheeks were beginning to sag. He would have low hanging jowls before he was fifty, no doubt.

Worst of all, he hated stories or anything the least bit fanciful. Before India, Esther never would have seen herself dancing with such a man. But now? Well, now she knew she deserved no better.

Her arms felt unusually heavy as her mind traveled back. The ballroom was glittering and lively, but none of the joy of the room seeped into her.

How could she enjoy herself, now, here? After the horrid things she'd said, and the most undesirable turn Lady Helen's life had taken as a result?

Still, she couldn't completely smother her enjoyment. She did so love to dance.

She was truly a horrid person for taking so much delight in her own situation when she'd been the cause of another's misfortune.

"You seem rather more downcast this evening than you were last we spoke," Lord Copeland said, his voice monotone as usual.

The next turn provided Esther with a few moments time to think over her response. "I am afraid I am suffering from a little headache this evening." Hopefully that would work—it would account for her mood without inviting him to pry into the truth of her melancholy.

"I am very sorry to hear that," Lord Copeland said. "After this set, let us find you a more comfortable chair than the one you previously occupied." He was a considerate gentleman, then. Esther felt only guilt for dancing with such a man.

The last of the set moved by as though Esther was only half present. Her head and heart seemed to be warring with one another, much as they had since her return to England. Her head proclaimed there was simply too much to enjoy to be bothered with any other thoughts. All the while, her heart seemed to beat a steady rhythm of guilt and shame.

The last notes of the dance faded from the room. Esther curtsied and Lord Copeland bowed. As she stood up straight once more, a man in a dark jacket caught her eye. He was standing near the doorway, a little apart from the rest of the crush. Blood left her face as her focus narrowed; suddenly she was aware of no one else but him.

Quintin—*her* Quintin—was here.

And, gracious, but he looked handsome. Sandy waves of hair and the bluest eyes. He wore a dark blue vest tonight, paired with a charcoal suit and a brilliant white ballroom cravat; he was quite enough to make any woman swoon.

Heaven help her, what was she to do?

He would know. One look at her and he'd know she wasn't all right. He'd know something awful had happened in India; she'd barely been able to keep it from him when they had spoken at his sister's wedding.

A hand took hold of hers. Esther startled at the unexpected touch.

"Lady Esther," Lord Copeland said, though she didn't look his way. "Is your headache worse? You seem suddenly pale."

Esther finally forced her eyes to leave Quintin. Lord Copeland had followed her gaze toward the ballroom doors, but they hadn't stopped on Quintin. Fortunately, he hadn't quite made out the focus of her stare.

She couldn't face Quintin. Not now. She'd have to speak with him eventually, but if only she could postpone it a bit longer. Surely she'd have a bit more nerve another day.

Drat, she *was* a coward.

"You know," she said, resting her hand atop Lord Copeland's arm. "I find I would dearly like some lively conversation just now. Is perhaps the friend you spoke of the other day here? You said his name was Lord Devon, I believe? You made him sound quite the wit." She gave him the brightest smile she could manage. She needed to try harder to not appear so out of sorts.

"He is here." Lord Copeland turned her blessedly away from the ballroom doors and toward a distant wall. "I would be delighted to introduce you. Though, perhaps you would allow me to claim a second dance first? The midnight waltz, perhaps?" He said it all very straightforwardly, as though they were discussing the weather or how they preferred their potatoes cooked.

Esther flattened the sigh that tried to break free. Lord Copeland was a bore. She already knew that about him. It shouldn't surprise or disappoint her. "Of course, my lord. I would be honored." At least that was one dance during which she wouldn't have to worry about Quintin.

As they moved through the room, however, all Esther could manage to feel was disgrace. She'd stooped to hiding from Quintin. Quintin, who'd been her childhood confidant and closest friend. But then, considering who she had learned herself to be in India, could she truly expect much better?

CHAPTER 3

*Q*uintin pushed his way into the ballroom. He carefully looked over each and every group of people he passed. A few acquaintances of his greeted him, but Quintin didn't stop long to speak with any of them. He'd had it on good authority that Esther would be present tonight. If that was the case, where was she?

A light laugh caused his step to pause mid-stride. Esther was in the center of the largest flock of gentlemen Quintin had ever seen. Perhaps he should call them a bevy of gentlemen, though, since all their fobs rather reminded him of puffed up, male quail. Either that, or he should call them a murder of gentlemen, since their black suits did rather paint them like a bunch of crows. Quail or crows, their presence could very well spell the death of his hope.

Quintin, staying close to the back wall, meandered around and closer to the group, stopping once he had view of Esther's face.

She was smiling her brilliant, exuberant smile, the one where her eyes shined as blue as a clear sky and her whole face lit up. She used to smile that way whenever they had gotten into mischief. A particular time came to mind; they had crossed a river atop a fallen log, and she'd slipped. Quintin had not-truly-accidentally fallen in after her. He loved that smile, almost as much as he loved her peaceful, all-is-right-in-the-world smile. That second smile was not one she assumed as often. Yet, in those rare moments when she did, he knew deep down that his life needed her as much as he needed breath.

Quintin wasn't sure who had pulled out Esther's exuberant smile this time, or how, but he couldn't deny the tempestuous mix of pleasure and jealousy he felt at the sight.

He ought to walk up to her.

Still, he hesitated. It wasn't as though Quintin *dis*liked society. It was only, he always seemed to disappear among all the other men in the room, and there were so very many around Esther just now.

Part of it was his own fault, he'd acknowledge that. He didn't often speak up or draw attention to himself. But, then again, it was almost always more interesting to listen to other people. He could keep company with his own thoughts whenever he wanted, but other people brought with them new ideas and perspectives. He'd much rather listen than be heard.

Besides, he'd long since learned if he spent too much time talking, he risked mentioning his imaginings of being a knight, or a roman god, or an adventurer crossing the wilds of Africa or South America. He'd only slipped up twice since he'd first attended Eton as a boy—but both situations had been so horrid, he'd never even come close to risking such a slip up again. Ever since, he'd kept himself along the walls of the dance room, in the furthest corner at supper parties, and always strived to remain very, very quiet.

Esther laughed. The sound was as sweet as fresh milk. He couldn't stop his own smile. She could always make him smile.

He truly needed to go up to her. Needed to speak to her, apologize for not arriving in London sooner, and let her know that he was here for her now. His hands clenched and unclenched over and over again.

Quintin took a deep breath, shut his eyes momentarily and *willed* himself to move forward.

His feet obeyed. The path between him and Esther had seemed

clear enough when he was against the back wall. However, now, as he crossed the room, it seemed every person around him was determined to move into his way. More than one gentleman stopped directly in his path only to talk to another. Several ladies bustled by, necessitating he stop and allow them to pass.

By the time he neared the circle of gentlemen, Esther was no longer there. Quintin stopped, uncertain what to do next. He lifted his head and looked about, searching each face.

Esther was dancing with a dark-haired man, one whom Quintin was suddenly disposed to disapprove of. The other gentlemen who had been surrounding Esther only moments ago stood in small clumps about Quintin. None seemed to notice his arrival.

"I've never seen a lady so lovely," one whispered to his companion.

"Nor I," the second responded.

Quintin's insides twisted even as the dancers swirled about the floor.

"Lord Copeland seems quite taken with her," the first spoke again. "If he secures her hand, he will be a lucky man indeed."

The music pounded against Quintin's head. Secure her hand? Were she and this Lord Copeland so connected already? The voices around Quintin swam together until he couldn't make out any distinct voice. The bodies swam as well, blurring until their colors were mere swipes of a wide brush, without detail or distinction. All he could see was Esther, smiling as she danced with a well-togged gentleman.

That must be the rumored Lord Copeland.

Could he truly be too late?

Years and years of waiting and working and hoping, and now it seemed all for naught.

The dance ended, none too soon. Quintin didn't allow his hesitancy to get the better of him again and he moved quickly toward the direction Lord Copeland was leading Esther. He walked up to them just as they were reaching the open doors which led to a back terrace.

"Good evening, Lady Esther," he said. At least his steady tone didn't betray him.

She stared at him, beautiful eyes slowly widening. "Quintin," she whispered.

A small bit of hope lit once more inside him—her tone sounded almost as happy to see him as he was to see her.

Then her brow dropped, and she leaned back ever so slightly. Not enough that anyone else would notice, but Quintin didn't miss it, and it was like a knife in his ribs.

There *was* something wrong.

Only, he hadn't the faintest idea what it might be. Was she upset he hadn't been there the very week she'd made her bows?

"Lord Quintin," Esther said, most formally as she gave an equally formal curtsy. "May I introduce you to Lord Copeland."

Quintin moved his eyes from Esther to the gentleman beside her. His eyebrows lifted. He'd been upset that she was standing up with someone else, but now that he got a better look at Lord Copeland his nerves eased. The man had to be almost two decades Esther's senior.

The introductions were quick. Quintin wholly wished the man would take himself off and allow him to speak with Esther uninterrupted. Instead, the man asked about Quintin's family and estate. Quintin felt obliged to return the interest and asked about Copeland's family as well. Boring man was quite well connected it seemed, and heir to a title; not third in line, as Quintin was.

Quintin had never been bothered by the knowledge that he was not in line for a title. Yet, there was something in the pointed way Lord Copeland spoke of his own title that left Quintin unsure of the man's motives.

Finally Quintin could stand the pointless conversation no longer. "Lady Esther, would you perhaps stand up during the next dance with me?" Dances provided only the briefest moments for conversation, but at least it was more than Copeland was allowing him now.

Esther didn't meet his eye, her gaze instead roving about the ballroom behind him. "I am sorry, but I believe my dance card is quite full."

Quintin swallowed, trying to hide his acute disappointment. He should have known the past four years would have changed her as much as it had him. Had he been a fool to think she still cared about the promises they'd shared beneath that willow tree? Did she even remember the incident?

"Of course," he said, though his tone was not as steady as before. Curses, he needed to leave before he found himself the center of ridicule. A man didn't fall apart when a lady could not dance with him; of course, such was no doubt purported by men who hadn't already lost their heart over a decade before. "Of course," he said again. He couldn't think of anything else to say.

With a bow, he took a small step back, then glanced back up at her.

Esther was smiling at Copeland again. Though, Quintin could easily detect a bit of something in her green eyes. Bleakness? Sadness?

Something was wrong in Esther's life. From that brief glimpse of her eyes, he knew it. It could be she didn't care for him any longer, or it could be something else entirely. He wasn't sure. But there *was* something wrong.

Esther and Copeland swept by him and continued their path out toward the night air. Copeland seemed a perfect gentleman, if a bit dull. Still, Quintin would have known if Esther wished to be rid of him. That didn't seem to be her wish at all. Copeland didn't seem to be the cause of Esther's doldrums, so Quintin let them go.

Was he, himself, the problem?

Quintin watched them through the doorway as they paused on the terrace. Whatever was bothering her, Esther wasn't allowing it to stop her from enjoying Copeland's company.

Quintin was used to being forgotten almost the moment he left someone's presence. But Esther had always been the one person who had never forgotten him, the one person who always looked back in hopes of seeing him.

Only now, it seemed she had forgotten him as well.

CHAPTER 4

*H*e was going to find her out. Already, after only a few minutes in each other's presence at the ball last night, Quintin acted as though he knew something was wrong. Esther reached for a tea cake, willing her mind to stay focused on the two women who were visiting. She and Mother were at-home today and had not known a moment of quiet. Normally Esther would have been delighted with all the company, but this morning she had a sour taste out of her mouth that she couldn't shake.

Esther leaned back in her seat, ready to place the newly chosen tea cake beside her cup. Another bit of cake already rested there, the one she only now remembered picking up not five minutes before. Oh, drat. Now Mrs. Trumbull and her daughter, Miss Charlotte, were bound to think her a pig. Ah, well, there was nothing for it now. She pushed the second piece of cake onto her plate and tried, again, to pay attention to the conversation.

"I did so enjoy the theater the other night," Miss Charlotte said in her quiet, although nasally voice. She didn't look up as she spoke and seemed to lean back and away the moment she was finished with her sentence.

"So did I," Esther said, taking a small bite of cake. The sooner she ate her unintentionally overloaded plate down, the better. "Did you happen to see Lord Brummel there?"

Miss Charlotte blushed. Esther had thought there might be something between her and Lord Brummel. At least, she was fairly certain there *would be* if only Miss Charlotte wasn't so terribly down cast and Lord Brummel wasn't so terribly quiet around ladies. In many ways, Miss Charlotte reminded Esther of Lady Helen. She, too, had been so very shy.

Shame, raw and biting, flooded Esther. She blinked many times, wishing the horrid emotion would, for once, leave her in peace.

"You know," Esther lowered her own voice so that Mother and Miss Charlotte's mother were less likely to overhear, "I do believe he's quite taken with you." Lord Brummel was highly spoken of wherever he went. Perhaps—just perhaps—Esther could make some sort of amends by helping this woman.

Miss Charlotte glanced at Esther with wide eyes, then dropped her gaze once more to her lap. "Really?" It was a hopeful, nearly strangled reply.

Poor dear—hadn't anyone ever told her how lovely she was? Or how kindhearted? Why, any man would be quite blessed to have Miss Charlotte as a wife.

"Yes." Esther pressed on. "Between you and me, I have seen him watching you at more than one assembly."

"He hardly ever says a word to me," Miss Charlotte said even as her shoulders slumped yet further. The act brought Lady Helen strongly to mind. Esther clamped her jaw tight in an effort to keep the guilt away. It didn't help.

"Do you speak much to him?" she asked, hoping her voice didn't sound as strangled as it felt.

"Oh no, I couldn't ... I wouldn't dream of . . ."

Gracious, these two were so alike that they may never realize it. If only there had been a Lord Brummel in India, everything may have been different. At least, it might have been for Lady Helen. But then, without Lady Helen available to take the fall, Esther probably would have found herself in a far worse situation.

Would it have been worse, however, than the shame she constantly felt now?

Esther pursed her lips. She was so tired of being haunted by India and the scandal she'd caused—the pain she'd inflicted on another woman. She placed her teacup on the low table in front of her and turned more fully toward Miss Charlotte. She would think no more of the past, and instead help this woman find happiness.

"I do believe a little encouragement would go a long way," Esther said.

Miss Charlotte blushed all the brighter. "Lady Esther," she breathed, sounding somewhat appalled.

"Oh, I don't mean anything untoward," Esther hurried on. "Only, smile a bit when he catches your eye. Or let him know that you *do* wish him to say something to you."

Miss Charlotte was silent for a moment and perfectly still. Esther almost envied the other woman's ability to hold so completely still; she certainly never could manage to do so. Even sitting for two hours during their at-home, regardless of the neighbors and friends bustling in and out, was a bit of a stretch for her. No doubt, if she had even an ounce of Miss Charlotte's peaceful demeanor, her nurse maid and governess would have been imminently happier.

"I suppose," Miss Charlotte said at last, "I suppose I could ... smile." Miss Charlotte smiled softly, almost as though she was testing out the idea. She truly was a beautiful woman.

"Yes," Esther said emphatically. "I think that is exactly what he needs to see."

"Charlotte," Mrs. Trumbull called. "What has you grinning like a baboon?"

The smile disappeared immediately. "Nothing, Mother."

Once both mothers were busy speaking to one another again, Esther leaned in once more, keeping her voice whisper-quiet. "It's what Lord Brummel needs to see; just apparently not your mother."

Charlotte chuckled softly. A soft sort of pleasure eased the constant pain in Esther's chest. Why had she not thought of it before? She could not go back and make things right with Lady Helen, as that woman was still in India and Esther now in England. However, maybe she could make amends in a roundabout sort of way by helping others instead. England already boasted so many debutantes this season, and there were guaranteed to be more. Soon, London, like a river in spring, would swell and overflow its banks.

Esther may have ruined Lady Helen's chances of a pleasant life, but could she not see to it that other women did not suffer the same fate? She had no idyllic notion that helping other women would somehow redeem her of past sins. But maybe it *would* ease the pain in her heart.

Soon Miss Charlotte and her mother bid adieu and left. Esther promised to visit them next week and Miss Charlotte seemed happy with the idea. The more Esther thought on her new plan, the more she liked it. There were many women in London just now who could use a bit of encouragement, and Esther was determined to provide just that.

With the room empty of all except herself and her mother, Esther strolled easily over to a table tucked beside a large window. One of her watercolors was framed and sitting atop the wooden surface. Perhaps she would finally pull her paints out today. She hadn't held a brush since returning from India. Painting was the one and only activity during which she could sit still comfortably for more than ten minutes.

Except, every time she'd tried since returning to London, she'd found that nothing flowed from her fingers as it once had. She'd simply stared at either the paper or canvas until she'd finally packed it all up once more. After a few weeks, she'd stopped getting the paint out altogether.

A manservant entered the parlor and bowed, announcing yet more visitors. Esther turned her back on her small watercolor. Perhaps the manservant would bring in some other young woman who needed a friend. That, at least, she could handle.

"Lady Cassandra Southcott, the Countess of Sutters, Lady Venetia Lockhart, and Lord Quintin Lockhart."

Esther felt all her previous thrill at this new plan shrivel up at the sound of her Quintin's name. He'd come to call on her?

She'd only just settled her equilibrium after their brief conversation at the ball last night. Perhaps if she stayed focused on her new plan of helping other women, she could stay calm even in his presence.

The ladies walked through the door first. Married life must be suiting Cassandra, for she smiled more radiantly than Esther could ever remember her doing before. Venetia looked well; anytime the youngest Lockhart was healthy it was a blessing. They both wore lovely dresses—Cassandra in Pomona green and Venetia in lavender.

Mother hurried forward, greeting both Lockhart sisters with a hug. They immediately began chatting happily. Though Esther could hear the pleasant tones of their voices, her brain couldn't seem to make sense of any of the words. Slowly she stood but remained near the settee.

Quintin walked in.

He was not so finely dressed as he had been last night at the ball, yet he looked every bit as handsome in a dark blue jacket with a fashionable, gold-topped walking stick in one hand. She'd noticed even before her trip to India that he'd grown to enjoy dressing in the peak of fashion. Not that he ever looked a fop or dressed outlandishly. But, when one stopped to notice, it was clear he took pleasure in dressing well.

For a childhood crush, she certainly had chosen well. So many of her friends who'd had hidden *tendres* for boys when they were young were only too glad that, after those boys turned to men, they'd kept their feelings to themselves. Her Quintin, however, was neither plain nor prone to roundness about the middle.

His gaze met hers the moment he walked into the room. Esther felt herself smile; how could she not? Seeing him again was like returning to the fields behind her family's country home. It was like sea bathing during the hottest of autumn days. It was like the warmth of a favorite blanket during a snow fall.

But also, it was unlike anything else at all.

There was simply nothing *exactly* like being with her Quintin. She saw him, and she saw the best parts of her childhood. Only, now, those memories were tainted with the knowledge of what she'd done, with the realization of who'd she'd become.

"I thought," Cassandra said, loud enough for the whole room to hear, "that we might take a turn about your small garden in the back. The weather is quite fine today and it ought to be enjoyed before winter reminds us it's not yet over."

"Excellent notion," Mother agreed. A servant was sent to fetch their pelisses and soon they moved out of doors.

Esther didn't say a word, and neither did Quintin. Yet, after only a few minutes they found themselves walking along the small garden path, side by side. Mother, Cassandra, and Venetia were all several steps ahead, no doubt with the specific design of granting her and Quintin some privacy.

Quintin couldn't seem to take his eyes off her when he'd first entered the parlor; however, now he seemed determined to look at anything *but* her. Proof he knew something was wrong.

"I was surprised to see you at the ball last night," she said at length.

"I can explain." His tone made it evident this was not going to be a casual conversation.

Normally, Esther was quite eager to delve into more forward conversations and leave the weather and simpering gossip behind. But this time, her stomach only rolled with nervous anticipation.

"I . . ." Quintin started, but then immediately paused. His step slowed and he angled his head her direction, not exactly looking at her, but clearly speaking only to her all the same. "I had no idea you'd made your bows. Please forgive my not being present when you did. I was under the apparently misguided impression that you would not be presented for several weeks yet."

"I had thought that as well, but you know my mother. She quite suddenly got it into her head that we should come as soon as possible and so come we did." The many tête-à-têtes she and Quintin had shared over the years came back to her with stunning force; gracious, but she did so enjoy speaking with her Quintin. "Between you and me, I think Mother missed the varied society of London. India was not so diverting for her."

"I am glad you have returned." Quintin's words came out slow.

She was glad, too. Though, she had to admit to herself, she was more glad to be rid of India and to leave it all behind her than she was glad to be back in London. How sad that even seeing Quintin again was eclipsed by leaving Lieutenant Fallow and Lady Helen behind.

Someone as horrid as she did not deserve such a good man as Quintin.

"How does Cottonhold fair?" she asked, wishing her guilt would leave her be.

His face fell and he shook his head. "Not well, I'm afraid. I study the numbers day and night. I work beside many of my tenants. Yet . . ." He shook his head again, more vehemently this time. "There must be *something* I'm missing. Nothing seems to ever work."

"Have you tried asking other landowners what they've done in similar situations?"

He glanced over at her with an alarmed expression. "Of course not."

She frowned. "Why not?" If he needed help, no doubt there was someone out there who'd been through the same ordeal and knew a thing or two. "I know several of my father's acquaintances have struggled with their estates from time to time."

"They may be your father's acquaintances, but they are not mine. I am nothing to them, so why would they help me?"

"Do not cast yourself down so very low. Moreover, do not assume the worst of those whom you have not yet met." Quintin seemed far from convinced, so Esther pressed on. "Surely it would not hurt to speak with one or two men whom you feel might be willing to give advice. You never know what you may learn."

"I'll think about it," he said softly. "I may speak easily enough with my tenants, but I must admit to finding it much harder to speak with other gentlemen of the peerage." Glancing her way, Quintin shot her a half smile.

Esther's heart flipped.

No one's smile had ever made her heart react so. Not even Quintin's when they were children. He'd always been a dear friend to her. But sometime between then and now—she couldn't rightly say when, it had come on so slowly—Esther had grown to want Quintin as more than a friend.

Only now, she wasn't so sure.

"You know," Esther began, though even those two words were unusually difficult to get out. "I often think of our many adventures as children."

Quintin's voice stayed soft. "As do I."

"We did so many silly, childish things back then." Back when the world was simple, only villains did bad things, and they could pretend at being heroes who set it all to right. Heroes never did anything to hurt another. Heroes never passed their struggles off to someone else. Esther blinked several times.

Quintin was silent.

How long until he learned of her shame?

"I feel these past few years have rather changed us both," she explained before clamping her mouth shut. She would soon be telling him the whole story if she kept this up. He'd always been so easy to talk to and she'd bared her sole to him more than once. But she'd been a girl then. Surely, as a grown woman she could hold her tongue.

The silence stretched out until it was almost unbearable. "I know I have changed," Esther said. Anything to fill the hole that was growing between them. "I saw the most amazing elephants in India."

Quintin continued walking by her side, but he said nothing.

She'd always been aware of his tendency toward silence around other people, but he'd rarely been so around her. It was more unnerving than she had expected.

"Did you know they paint them?" she continued, hoping her own fake enthusiasm for the topic would draw some of the same out of him. "The colors are amazing. Yellow and purple. And they have ever so much red fabric there."

Gracious, it was hard to carry on a conversation on her own. All the more so because she was in no way blind to the fact that Quintin was ill-at-ease—something they'd never once been around each other.

"Rugs, robes . . ." She kept talking.

If only he'd say something.

At least they weren't discussing what she'd done in India. "I've never seen so much red in all my life. It makes me wonder what other things I've missed out on. I've always had a clear idea of what I wanted to do in life but now I find myself wondering if I shouldn't explore other options."

Quintin stopped in the path. Slowly, he turned until he faced her fully. He held his walking stick in one hand, positioned directly in front of him, his other hand resting atop it. "What exactly are you saying, Esther?"

Like she knew. She was only babbling to keep him from learning of what she'd done. So long as he only thought of elephants and red rugs whenever her trip to India came up, she was safe.

"I'm only telling you of India." The lie hurt as it left her mouth.

Quintin's brow dropped; he wasn't falling for it. "We may be grown, but you can still be frank with me."

She *could* be frank, but then he'd call off and never speak with her again.

"Are you saying," his voice was even quieter than before, "that you no longer wish to pursue a connection between us?"

Of course she wished for a connection between them—desperately so. She wanted it so much it hurt. But the truth was, she'd been the catalyst to a terrible scandal and another woman had paid the price. How could she continue on after that, happily wedding a man she cared so much for?

But gracious, he looked so very dejected. She hadn't wanted to break his heart. Unfortunately, the truth had just as much potential to break him as a lie. Esther reached out and laid a hand against his chest.

He shuddered beneath her touch, sending a wave of tingles up her own arm. Something ignited inside her and suddenly all she wanted was to wind her arms around him, forget India, and promise to always be his.

She couldn't, though. Her heart, despite its cries for Quintin, also demanded she punish herself for her weakness. Such was only fair.

"Quintin, you were the best friend a little girl could have ever asked for." If nothing else, he needed to know that she had always cherished his friendship.

Instead of the bit of light she hoped to spy in his eyes, his face grew slack. "But we've supposedly changed?"

He may not have. Quintin was probably every bit the good-hearted individual he'd been as a boy. *She* was the one who wasn't without fault. "Doesn't everyone?" she hedged, dreading the idea of telling the truth. "Can you honestly say you are the exact same little boy who dreamed of slaying dragons and exploring the jungles of South America?"

"Yes; I am older," Quintin said. "But I'm not *that* different."

"Well, I am." The words felt final. Of course he expected her to be as guileless as she'd been as a girl. As such, it would be better for them both to end things now.

Quintin rocked back. Hurt was etched in each line of his face, in the tenseness across his shoulders, and the way he clutched to the walking stick. No doubt, were his gloves off, she'd see the white of his knuckles.

Esther rested a hand on his arm. "Quintin, I am sorry."

He pulled back abruptly, facing the garden path once more. The moment he broke the connection between them, she felt it. The separation was like a deep ache—one that felt both heartbreaking and just. She deserved no less; it was just awful that Quintin, too, had to hurt because of her.

"It's like you said." Quintin put one foot in front of the other, continuing their walk down the path. "We were but children then. And everyone knows children do foolish things."

CHAPTER 5

*T*he fire crackled and the large piece of wood resting in the center of the fireplace cracked in two. Quintin didn't so much as blink.

Four days.

Four days since his conversation with Esther. He probably ought to consider her *Lady* Esther now. He no longer had the right to call her anything else. She, it would seem, had grown up and no longer wanted anything to do with him.

A knock sounded from his bedchamber door. Probably one of the maids with supper. He'd taken nearly all his meals in his room since that horrid turn about the Collingwoods' garden. Blast that garden.

"Enter," he called, not bothering to move from the deep slump he was currently in.

"There you are."

That wasn't one of the maids. Quintin lifted his head out of the hand it had been resting against and stared at the door. He couldn't see much. When had the room gotten so dark? After watching the fire for so long, bright orange spots danced across his vision.

"Venetia?" he asked, blinking the last of the spots away. What in the blazes was she doing here? "You and Cassandra left London day before last."

"Cassandra left London." She padded across the room and took the chair across from him. "I felt you may need some company for a little longer. If you hadn't stayed hidden in here for so long, you might have known that before now." Her eyes roved about the walls and furnishings.

"So, is a man's room rather bland compared to a woman's?" Whatever she stayed around for—and he had a pretty good idea— he wasn't ready to discuss it.

"Yes, but mostly I was thinking that of all my brothers, your room has changed the least."

"How would you know?" Once they had left the nursery, even though they were still young, the girls did not go in the boys' rooms and the boys certainly had not ventured into the girls'.

"Did you know," she said with a lopsided grin. "That if you go through that door"—she pointed at the servant's entrance to the side of the hearth—"go down the hallway to your left, and take the third door, you'll end up in my room?"

"You know the servants' hallways?"

"I know all the hallways. In all Father's houses. What do you think I do to entertain myself when Mother orders me to stay in bed for days on end?"

Despite himself, Quintin felt a smile tug at his mouth. "I bet you can't say the same thing for Cottonhold. You've only visited once."

"And I was stuck in bed twice, both times for nearly a week."

Quintin shook his head. "If Penelope only knew."

"Don't you dare tell her, or she'll start chaining me to the bed post."

Quintin chuckled at the thought, his gaze returning to the fire. It was quite low, now that he truly noticed it. Standing, he pulled the cord to ring for a servant. His valet appeared almost instantly, and Quintin requested more firewood.

Once the fire was stoked and brilliant once more, he returned to sitting.

"She turned you down, didn't she?" Venetia said.

"Is it that obvious?"

Venetia let out the strangest, unladylike guffaw he'd ever heard.

"Come now," he said. "No need to do it brown."

"I'm sorry. It's just so plainly obvious. You always hide when you're upset."

"I do not," he stated firmly. Because he didn't.

Venetia speared him with pursed lips and eyes that clearly said, "Oh, yes you do."

Well, maybe he hid sometimes. He just hated being out and with people when he was puzzling over something on the inside.

"And you stop dressing in the peak of fashion," Venetia said, pointing a finger toward Quintin's lack of jacket and faded breeches.

"I dress however I feel like dressing. I'm no peacock." Folding his arms, he leaned back in his chair. Since Penelope—his stepmother and Venetia's real mother—wasn't around, he slouched once more. "She said we've both changed and that we couldn't possibly be right for each other anymore."

"I'm sorry to hear that."

"Not nearly as sorry as I was," he muttered. Why had Esther been so quick to dismiss his suit? So sure that, since she'd changed, that they wouldn't do for one another?

"What are you going to do now?" Venetia asked.

Quintin only shrugged. His estate was hounding him day in and day out, and he'd only been gone a week. Perhaps he should just return. Esther had clearly avoided him at the ball and then all but kicked him out when he'd come to call.

"Quintin Lockhart." Venetia's tone was hard. "If you give up this easily, I swear I will never forgive you."

He grunted and rolled his head to the side to face her. "You haven't even come out yet, Venetia, and won't for another year. What do you know of such things?"

Ah, lud. Had the words really come out of his mouth? He knew regret the moment they filled the space between him and his sister.

Her brow dropped low and her jaw tightened. Standing, she moved over closer, towering over him. "I can't believe you…" Her hands were in fists by her sides and her voice grew louder with each word. "How dare…I'm not some naive child."

"Venetia, I'm sorry."

She stomped toward the door, flinging it open. "Enjoy your solitude." She slammed it behind herself, the resounding thud echoing about the otherwise silent room.

Quintin groaned and shut his eyes. He should have known better. Venetia had become quite sensitive to being treated as a child these past few years. As the youngest of the Lockhart siblings, he supposed she was often disregarded. He knew that. He should have thought before he spoke. He hadn't meant to imply she was naive. Only, well, that he was hurting himself.

Blast, she was right, too. He was acting as though there was nothing he could do about Esther. He was acting as though giving up was the only course of action available to him. Standing, he began pacing in front of the fire.

He didn't understand why Esther had said the things she had. In a lot of ways it was like that one time he'd try to convince her to climb the enormous tree by the vicarage. At least it was enormous to a young boy. They'd climbed trees together before and she'd never hesitated. For what felt like weeks he'd tried to convince her that it was the best climbing tree in all the county.

Quintin paused in his pacing. That's what her eyes had reminded him of. They had reminded him of those days when she'd refused to climb the tree. How had he finally gotten her to agree to climb up after him? He could remember the moment, the victory he'd felt looking down on her smiling face, the hours they'd spent that glorious afternoon among the leaves and branches. He smiled at the memory.

He placed both hands against the mantel and leaned heavily against it. Was he a fool to think that even a small bit of that happiness could still be theirs? The way she'd looked at him while they walked through the garden was so very much like when she'd refused to climb the large tree.

"Come on, it's an amazing tree."

Memories from over a decade ago surfaced, strong and vivid.

"Just try it. It's not too far off the ground."

Esther, in pigtails and a cream dress, wordlessly shook her head.

Was she ever going to climb the tree? Frustration bubbled inside his small chest. "But why?" he yelled.

Esther's lip began to shake, and her eyes filled up with tears. She pointed out past the tree trunk. Quintin followed the direction, his gaze landing on the rows of old headstones.

"I don't want the ghosts to get me." Esther's voice floated up to him, soft and broken.

Quintin swung his leg over the thick branch he was straddling and dangled from it instead. Letting go, he fell to the ground. He hurried over to Esther and took her still pointing hand in his.

"The ghosts won't get you." He puffed his chest out. "I won't let them."

That was it. Quintin blinked several times. He hadn't labeled what Esther had been feeling back then as fear, but he'd recognized it, nonetheless. Was she afraid now? If so, then of what? Of marrying him? That was a humbling thought.

Or perhaps she was afraid of marriage in general. The law dictated that a woman was wholly at the mercy of her husband. No finances were exclusively hers, and she was not allowed to go against her husband's will in any way. Once a woman married, she had to do his bidding.

But surely she didn't believe he would be a tyrant of a husband. What *had* happened in India? What had she seen or experienced that suddenly made her unwilling to accept his suit?

He pushed off the mantel and scrubbed at the stubble along his chin. Or perhaps he was just being a conceited popinjay. Perhaps she'd met too many handsome, well-connected, fascinating men and she couldn't see herself settling down with someone as quiet and forgettable as he.

Either way, he wasn't going to give up this easily. Quintin respected Esther's wish for some space and he wasn't about to stalk up to her father and demand he give him her hand. But he wasn't going to walk away either. First thing tomorrow, he'd see what he could learn about her family's trip to India. Then, he'd keep finding times to run into her without pressing the connection. Hopefully, if he didn't rush her, Esther would realize she could still trust him, just like she had when they were children.

Whatever the cause of Esther's fear, he was determined to learn the truth.

CHAPTER 6

*E*sther pushed the boiled potatoes about her plate. They were as colorless and flavorless as ever. It was rather a pity they had not thought to bring Cook to India with them. Perhaps she might have picked up a little more gumption when it came to spices and seasoning.

"Are you all right, my dear?" Mother asked from across the table.

"I am fine," Esther said, without thought. She'd grown up with bland food, but it was ever so much more difficult to swallow now that she'd tasted the exotic and varied flavors of India.

"Your father will no doubt be holed up in his book room from now until supper," Mother said, her tone a bit tense. For having been married nearly two decades Esther wondered that her mother had not grown to expect her father's indisposition toward constant society. "I do not feel it wise to have another at-home today," she continued, tossing Esther a warning look. "One does not want to look desperate."

"I quite agree." But not because she cared about looking or not looking desperate. Esther was not in the mood for company. Every-

thing—every ball and opera—had seemed as bland as Cook's potatoes since her last conversation with Quintin.

Had she expected him to call on her again the very next day?
She didn't believe so. Yet, less than twenty-four hours after their
conversation she had begun to feel the biting sting of his absence.
Hadn't she asked for space, though? She'd been so certain that
breaking her connection with Quintin was the right thing to do.
Now that she'd taken the first step in that direction, she didn't feel
any better for it. It was all very confusing.

"Dear?" Mother's voice came from further away than it had
before. Esther glanced up. Mother stood near the breakfast room
door.

"Are you not coming?" she asked.

Esther glanced down at her plate. She hadn't eaten much, as the
many bites of food still before her indicated. Yet, she couldn't seem
to force any of them down.

Esther pushed away from the table and stood. "Actually, I think
I would like to take a turn outside." Perhaps some fresh air would
clear her mind.

"In this weather?"

Was the weather bad? She hadn't really noticed that morning.
Esther turned and looked out of a window. No snow fell and only
traces of it were still visible in patches. Nonetheless, it looked cold.

"I shall wear my warm pelisse," Esther said. "And I shall only
go to the stables and back."

Mother pursed her lips, and Esther could see her turning over
the idea in her mind. Eventually she nodded. "Very well. Only be
sure to turn back to the house if you feel yourself getting too cold."

"Of course, Mother." Esther turned toward a different door.
Now that the idea of going outside had entered her mind, it felt the
perfect remedy for her unsettled mind.

"Oh, and Esther?" Mother called just before she left the room.

Esther turned back expectantly.

"I don't know what it is you told that Lockhart boy the other day," Mother continued, "but I am glad you sent him off. You can do far better than a third son."

Hot indignation rose up, burning Esther's chest. She clenched her skirt tightly within both hands. She'd always known Quintin wasn't Mother's favorite, but she'd never dreamed Mother would say something so horrid.

"Lord Quintin is a fine gentleman, Mother." He was ever so much more than simply "fine." He was considerate and felt deeply. He had kept ever so many of her confidences when they had been children and had always been there when she was scared.

Mother raised a single, thin eyebrow. "If that is true, then why did you send him away?" Without giving Esther time to respond, she glided from the room.

Left alone, Esther let out a very unladylike growl. Mother would never understand. She rarely did, and this was far more complicated a situation than Esther had ever found herself in before. Moving quickly toward the back doors, she had her warm things brought post haste. She needed some time alone to think.

Soon, she was traipsing out of doors. Though she was bundled quite well, the cold still found bits of openings around her neck and up her sleeves where it slunk in and chilled her skin.

Esther slumped a bit, pulling her pelisse yet closer to her. She stomped across the lingering snow and frozen grass. If her boots got a bit of mud on them, what did it matter? They were only boots after all. She had far heavier matters to worry over.

The stable was only a bit warmer than outside. Horses turned her way as she entered. She rubbed Lily Bay lightly on her nose. The nearly half dozen horses they'd brought when they'd come to London, as well as one horse she didn't recognize, stood before her. Father must have a visitor, and one who planned on staying long it would seem. That would account for the extra horse. There was a man she didn't recognize brushing down the horse as well.

His eyes landed on her and he bowed low, pulling on his forelock. A coachman or a groomsman, then. Drat him being here.

Esther had truly wanted to be alone. The memory of speaking with Quintin warred inside her with her memories of India. She couldn't seem to make them agree or fit together. Instead, they insisted on clashing about, each declaring they deserved more space than she could allot them.

Esther turned slowly. She didn't want to go back outside. The single bench along the garden path would no doubt be frigid. It was either here or the house and with Mother walking about, declaring Quintin was beneath them, Esther couldn't bear to be in the house just now. Her eye landed on a bit of wood—a ladder leading up to a loft above. That might just work.

She glanced back over at the manservant. His back was toward her as he brushed the unfamiliar horse, talking softly all the while. He must have sensed her desire for privacy and was willing to give it to her. Bless him. Drawing her skirts up so as not to trip, Esther hurried up the ladder.

The loft was even warmer than down by the horses. That was an unexpected blessing. Traces of hay littered the area, and several bales of it filled the far corner. But the area just about her was clear. Esther reached for a beam off to her right—there was no railing to keep one from falling—and stepped forward. The wood beneath her boot groaned loudly and buckled slightly. Esther's heart leapt and she skipped forward.

The wood over closer to the hay didn't complain in the least. She'd had enough complaints today, both from her mother and also from her own mind; she didn't need it from the floorboards as well. She found a bale that was chair height and sat upon it. The hay pricked against her pelisse, but the thick fabric prevented any of it from reaching her person.

Why had she told Quintin she needed space?

Because he *was* a gentleman and kind and all the wonderful things a man ought to be. Because someone like that would never understand what she'd done or why she'd done it. Sometimes she herself didn't understand. That realization that had come to her over and over again is what made her so desperate to keep Quintin from the truth.

Oh, how she wished she never had to marry at all. That would solve so many of her heartaches. If she were an heiress, or a peer in her own right, then she could simply state she was uninterested in marriage, quit London for good, and live alone, far from anyone she might inadvertently hurt. But it wasn't so simple. She needed the security and safety of a marriage; her parents could not support her indefinitely. Since she had no brothers, after her father passed, his wealth would go to a distant cousin, one she had no promise would not cast her out on the street.

Folding her arms, Esther leaned against another bale and rested her head in the folds of fabric. Though she did not fall fully asleep, Esther's mind returned to India—to one horrid evening in particular.

"Please, sir, we ought to return to the group," Esther said in a low voice.

Lieutenant Fallow laughed softly; it did not sound kind. "But why? The moon is so lovely tonight." He leaned in closer. "Do you not want to see how it looks from the ruins?"

Esther's heart pulsed loudly in her ears and she took a large step backward. "My mother will be wondering about me."

The lieutenant moved up close once more. "We won't be gone that long." His smile turned wide, wild almost.

Esther tried again to put space between them. Why had mother insisted she join the midnight picnic tonight? She had not even made her bows yet. Though, society in India cared little for such details; and by "society" she mainly meant the men in uniform who were everywhere they went.

If only Uncle had not chosen now to grow ill, then Mother would not have insisted they visit India in the first place. But it was too late for "if onlys" now.

"I must confess," she tried to keep her voice light, "I am getting a bit of a headache, and I have seen ever so many ruins since coming here." She felt certain he would only grow *more* blatant in his advances if he saw her fear, not less.

"Not with me, you haven't." He lifted a hand as though to cup it against her cheek.

Esther turned away; her blessed bonnet blocking his touch. It had been hot and sticky all day, but propriety had required she keep her bonnet on for the midnight picnic. Never had she been so thankful for social requirements.

Taking advantage of his momentary pause, Esther took a few steps back toward the rest of the party—a gathering of tables and chairs laid out across a small opening with tall candles lighting the space.

"I am not one for old buildings and crumbling stones," Esther lied, praying he would simply fall into step beside her instead of doing something much worse. "I do enjoy the company here in India though." If only she could get the lieutenant to enjoy someone *else's* company. He wasn't in any way infatuated with her, Esther knew. He was only looking for better connections. Her Uncle was his superior's superior, after all. Moreover, with her being not yet out, he probably saw her as young and easy prey.

She took another step. "I have met so many wonderful people here." No noise came from behind her. Why wasn't he following? If they could only return to the ring of candlelight, she was certain she would be safe once more.

Lieutenant Fallow's hand wrapped around her arm, squeezing her tight. Esther tried to cry out, but she suddenly couldn't make a sound.

"Listen." His voice was harsh. "I can't stay here. I hate the heat. I hate the people. I hate knowing my sister is left undefended against my father's schemes . . ." His eyes came into focus, as though he was seeing her again. Then his face went slack. He pried his fingers slowly, one by one, off her. He leaned back slightly, his jaw working. "You're my one chance to escape this inferno." He was breathing hard. Though he no longer held her, Esther could sense the erratic panic inside him.

"I don't see how I could . . ."

"You will marry me." The words came out hard, unbending. "Then you will tell your Uncle how much you hate it here. He cares for you. He'll see to it I'm posted back in England."

"Please, Lieutenant—" He blurred in front of her as tears filled her eyes.

"It's too late." No remorse colored his tone. "We've already been gone long enough for it to be noticed. As soon as the rest of the party has finished their tarts, someone will wander this way and find us."

No. She couldn't allow this. She simply could not marry him. She was going to marry Quintin. She'd known that—*wanted* that—since she was barely out of leading strings. This wasn't how her trip to India was supposed to end.

Esther blinked, sending several tears down her cheek. "You mustn't. Please." She took a step back. Perhaps if she slipped away and rejoined the party alone? But the lieutenant was right; it was likely rumors had already begun. Everyone had seen her walk off with him. Oh, why had Mother not stopped them?

Lieutenant Fallows, quick as a snake striking, took hold of her arm once more, this time around the wrist. "Stay here, and I won't have reason to hurt you."

Esther shook her head. She *could not* be forced to marry such a man. "There must be another way. Some other option."

Fallow looked past her, watching the party as they chatted and laughed among the candles. "I've tried everything. This is my last option."

"But, surely, if my uncle could send you back to England, he would have by now."

"As a single man, I'm bound to go wherever my superiors tell me to go. But once I'm married, that will change. Trust me, I've already thought this through."

His hand tightened around her wrist until his grip was painful.

Esther sucked in a shaking breath. There had to be a way out of this. Anything to avoid being shackled to this man for life. "Surely there is someone else you'd prefer to spend your life . . ."

Lieutenant Fallow shook his head. "Your connection with your uncle is all I need."

The brush rustled from off to Esther's left. Someone would find them. Any minute now and all would be ruined. Forever.

"Lady Helen Perry," Esther said brusquely.

"Excuse me?" His gaze dropped to her once more.

"Have you considered Lady Helen?"

"Why—"

"Her mother's half-brother is my uncle's superior." The words scraped against her tongue as she spoke them. Guilt, immediate and hot, filled her stomach. Still, this was her only chance. The only thing she could think of to escape. "If it's connections you're want- ing, she is a better candidate."

He watched her, thoughts clearly swirling about in his head. "I did not know."

"Her uncle is already stationed in England. I hear he has a soft spot for Lady Helen."

His jaw tightened. "It wouldn't work. Look at her." He threw his chin toward the party. In between a couple of large flowering bushes, Esther could see Lady Helen sitting demurely between two elderly matrons. "She's never alone. Never allowed to be called on." His gaze returned to her and his hand tightened once more. "You'll have to do."

"But she's so docile." She shouldn't be saying this. This was horrid and wrong. "Lady Helen would never go against anything you say. If you ask her to write to her uncle and beg to be brought back to England *with* her husband, she'll do it." Esther almost couldn't breathe. What was she saying? What was she doing? That poor, submissive woman didn't stand a chance against someone as determined as Lieutenant Fallow. Her whole frame felt on fire, heat from panic and desperation mixed with the burn of guilt and shame at her own words.

Lieutenant Fallow dropped her hand. "Perhaps you are right."

Not waiting for her reply, he pushed past her and strode, alone, back into the ring of candlelight. A sob broke from Esther, pushing painfully against her chest. She covered her hand with her mouth. What had she done?

Two months later, Esther attended the wedding of Lieutenant Fallow and Lady Helen. Never had a bride looked so miserable. There had been much gossip passed around about just how their unexpected connection had been formed. They'd known each other for months and yet had shown no interest. Then, quite suddenly, they were engaged. Some said he'd fought off a tiger for her and she'd lost her heart to him because of it. Others said they must have been secretly in love all this time. The meanest rumor of them all said Lady Helen imbibed in private and then threw herself at Fallow one night.

Immediately after Fallow had tried to force her into a marriage with him, Esther had told her Uncle the whole of the unfortunate affair, hoping he could save Lady Helen since she felt powerless to do so herself. But Uncle, sick and irritable, had only dismissed her accusations against Fallow. He claimed she'd misinterpreted the situation. Lieutenant Fallow was an upstanding soldier and Uncle would hear nothing else from her.

Sitting on the hard bench, with the stick of the Indian summer causing her dress to cling in all the wrong places, Esther could barely keep the tears at bay. Lady Helen didn't smile once during the ceremony. In that moment, listening to the preacher pronounce the unfit couple man and wife, Esther knew it was all her fault. She was the one who'd forced Lady Helen into this match as much as the lieutenant. No doubt, he'd cornered Lady Helen just as he had Esther. Shame and hatred at herself for what she'd done buried deep into Esther's chest, rooting itself in her stomach.

A woman who did that to another didn't deserve her own happy marriage, and certainly not with a kind man who thought her his faultless princess.

Over and over, that one thought circled around her head. It still circled her mind every time she saw or even thought of Quintin. She was weak and horrid and selfish. Walking away from Quintin now would hurt him. But, in the long run, being married to one such as her would hurt him far more.

CHAPTER 7

"*L*ady Esther? My lady?"

Esther squeezed her eyes yet more closed. She wasn't ready to get up. Wasn't ready to leave the hay loft, which had grown warmer as she dreamed.

"My lady?"

Muffled voices from below.

The creak of the ladder. "Lady Esther?"

Oh, all right. If Joan was going to continue calling her, then Esther might as well respond. She lifted her head. The space was darker than she expected. Evening would be here soon, it seemed. Esther blinked a few times. Her arms and neck were stiff, and she couldn't seem to shake a tightness in her chest that made breathing uncomfortable. No doubt, it was because of the memories she'd been reliving moments before.

"Pardon me, my lady." Joan appeared atop the ladder. "Her ladyship sent me to fetch you. It's time to get ready for tonight's ball."

"Yes, I'm coming." Esther turned her back to her lady's maid. The last thing she wanted right now was to attend a ball. Fresh shame churned inside her. How had she done something so horrid?

Even now, half a year later, she felt certain there was no forgiveness for her actions. She'd acted fully aware of the consequences to Lady Helen, and she'd spoken those blasted words regardless.

Esther placed her hands on a bale of hay, intending to push off it, but paused before doing so. She felt weak. Head to toe, it was as though she'd been drained of any strength. Her arms and legs felt as though they were sagging, lifelessly slumped atop the hay she was on.

"Let me help, my lady."

Esther heard Joan climb off the ladder and onto the loft, but she didn't turn or face her. She couldn't even seem to find the strength to lift her head. Why had she done it? Being forced to marry the lieutenant would have been awful—but it didn't justify forcing someone *else* to take her place.

"Come, my la—" Joan's words were drowned out by a deep, loud *crack* and she screamed.

Esther stood and whirled around. Joan was on the loft floor, crying and reaching toward her foot. Esther hurried over.

"Joan, are you all right?" She knelt down beside her abigail.

The floorboard beneath Joan's foot had given way and her foot had broken through. Esther scooted down toward the injured foot and pulled back a layer of skirt to get a clear look.

"Your foot is caught." Two halves of the broken floorboard pinned Joan's foot between them. Esther first wrapped a hand around Joan's foot—tugging only made Joan whimper—and then on either piece of wood—neither of which would budge.

"Oh, drat," Esther whispered. She turned toward Joan. "Do you think it's broken?"

Joan, face white and with tears streaking her cheeks, shook her head. "I can't rightly say, but I think not."

That, at least, was a blessing. "I can't seem to get you out. I'll have to go for help."

"No, please." Joan seemed near panic. "Don't leave me."

Esther worried her bottom lip. What was she to do? Joan looked so frightened Esther hated to leave her when she was undoubtedly in pain. But how was she to get help if she stayed here?

"Is the manservant still down there?" Esther asked, even as she scooted toward the loft edge.

"No," Joan said, then hiccupped a small bit of a sob. "He was taking his master's horse back out when I entered."

"That would have only been a few minutes ago. He probably hasn't gone far." Esther stood and hurried past Joan, toward the small loft window. It was chest high and so small she could only get her head out a short ways. The world around her looked gray and lifeless. Where was the manservant?

"Help!" Esther called out. Her voice echoed across the open field and toward the house which stood not too far away. "Someone please, we need help!"

A figure peered around the corner of the house. Esther squirmed around until she could get her arm out the window as well as her head and waved furiously. "This way!"

The figure, a man, bolted her direction. Esther tugged herself back inside. "It's all right, Joan. Help is on the way."

The man charged into the stable the next moment. He was quite fast to have arrived so quickly. Esther stood as close to the edge of the loft as she dared, keeping one hand on a beam to prevent herself from falling. The man was the servant, come with whomever was visiting with Father.

"Her foot fell through a floorboard," Esther explained as quick as she could push the words out. "I can't get her free."

The man climbed up the ladder and hurried over to Joan. "It's wedged in there well enough," he said as he looked over her foot. He looked up at Joan and smiled. "Don't worry. I know what to do. You'll be just fine."

Joan bit down on her lip—Esther got the impression she was trying hard not to cry further—and only nodded her head.

The manservant slipped back down the ladder and began rummaging around. Probably looking for a tool or something else necessary to free Joan. Esther left him to it and instead knelt by her abigail's head.

She lifted a hand and stroked back a bit of stray hair from the young woman's face. "It's going to be just fine, Joan. Don't worry. We'll have you out in no time at all."

"That's right." The man's voice came from the top of the ladder. He was back already. "In no time at all." In one hand he held a small saw.

Joan sucked in a shuddering breath. Esther patted her shoulder. "Truly, you will be just fine."

The man servant moved up close to Joan's foot. "The lady's right. You don't have to worry; I've done this sort of thing before." He placed the saw against one of the halves of the floorboard. Leaning heavily against the tool, he pulled it across the wood. A loud, sputtering moan filled the loft.

Though Esther sat directly beside Joan, she hoped the young woman would not feel her own shudders at the sound; if that blade slipped even the smallest bit, it could do serious damage. The manservant worked with precision and speed. The bit of wood between Joan's ankle and the saw began to shake visibly with each stroke of the saw.

Joan cried out. "It's hurting worse."

The man paused, breathing heavily. "It's only going to rub more painfully until it's cut free."

Joan let out a small whimper. Esther could only imagine what pain she must be experiencing right now. The jagged edge of floorboard had been pinching her ankle tight, and now it was rubbing it raw.

"Can I hold it still?" Esther asked, moving closer to Joan's ankle.

The man servant gave her a firm nod. "Hold it like this." He demonstrated, placing a hand on either side of the wood. There wasn't much to hold on to and with Joan's foot in the way it wasn't as though she could grab the wood, only keep it from moving about so much.

The man picked up the saw once more and placed the blade

back into the groove he'd been cutting. "Don't worry, miss. I'll not harm any of your fingers."

At the comment, Esther realized just how close her hands were to the blade. Even closer than Joan's foot. She swallowed and steeled herself. "Just finish quickly."

"That I will." The man servant's arm moved down with such force that the sound was near deafening. The wood vibrated beneath Esther's hands and Joan began crying softly once more. Again, the manservant cut down against the wood. She could feel it beginning to give underneath her left hand. He was almost fully through.

With a grunt, he pressed down and the wood fell out from beneath Esther's palms. The small piece, only a handspan in either direction, tumbled away and landed on the hay below with nothing but a *plat*.

Joan took in several, loud, long breaths. Esther rocked back, suddenly aware of how hard her heart was beating in her chest. The man gently, slowly turned Joan's foot around and pulled it out of the now enlarged hole. "There you are," he said softly, as though soothing a colt. "Free once more."

"Thank you," Joan said, her voice even softer than usual.

"I'm just glad I was about," he said, slipping an arm under her shoulders. "Now, let's get you down from here."

"And back into the house," Esther added. "We best send for the doctor right away so he can ascertain if your ankle is truly broken or not."

"Please, my lady," Joan said. "I am sure I will be quite fine now."

"Nonsense," Esther said. "I'm going to see to it that you have the rest of the day off and that a doctor takes a look at you before bed tonight." Now that she was certain Joan would be all right, Esther began to feel the effects of the ordeal pulling at her. The situation could have turned out far worse. "And thank you to you," she said to the manservant. "I, too, am glad you were nearby and available to help."

"Nothing to it, my lady," he said, bowing his head.

"Please, tell me your name." Esther said. After all they'd just gone through, it seemed ridiculous she didn't even know what to call him.

"Will Stanley, if you please," he said, bowing his head again. "Lord Dunn's groomsman and occasional driver."

"Then we are all blessed that Lord Dunn decided to call on my father today," Esther added, relief finally replacing the panic in her chest.

Joan nodded, her eyes moving to Will's and holding them. "Yes, very blessed indeed."

Joan smiled and Will smiled back.

CHAPTER 8

*Q*uintin moved about the large room, hands behind his back. The Garrisons must be imminently pleased; the room was full to bursting. It was quite a successful musicale if Quintin had ever seen one. Unfortunately, it only served to make it all the harder to tell if Esther was in attendance or not. After speaking with Venetia a few days prior, he'd determined to let Esther know two things. First, he wasn't going to rush her into any decisions. Second, they were still good friends and he was willing to listen if ever she wanted to talk. It was a loose and unnerving plan; there were so many things that could go wrong. Yet, it was all he had.

He reached the far side of the room and let out a small harrumph, drawing the raised brows of a few closely seated matrons. Of course, his plan would go much better if he could ever manage to be in the same room as Esther. Now that Penelope and Cassandra had left, he had no means of finding out which of the many gatherings taking place in London every night Esther would be attending. Granted, Venetia had stayed behind, but she wasn't even out yet. It wasn't as though she could go calling on her own and find out for him.

Another young woman took to the pianoforte; after a shallow curtsy, her fingers filled the room with music. Quintin leaned a shoulder against the wall. He knew of two balls, and another musicale, and the Thompson's were having several families over for cards tonight. Esther could be in attendance at any of those.

Of course, he could use this opportunity to do as Esther recommended and speak with a few other landowners about their tenants and the like. He'd very nearly done so yesterday but couldn't find the right opening in the conversation.

Besides, he wasn't nearly as interested in discussing his land with other gentlemen at the moment as he was discussing *anything* with Esther. If he didn't spot her soon, he would simply slip out, unnoticed, and try a different gathering. Sometimes, there were benefits to being the one no one noticed.

A side door opened, and Lord and Lady Harrington moved into the room, heads high. Quintin stood up straight, trying to see around them. Was she with her parents tonight? Surely, if Lord and Lady—

There she was. Dressed in white and primrose yellow, Esther glided in, wearing a soft smile for the people she passed. Her brown hair was up, small lavender flowers accentuating the many loops and curls. It still took his breath away to see what a gorgeous woman she'd grown to be. He'd always thought her pretty; even as a young boy, before he could form the words properly in his own mind, he had thought she was most pleasing to look at. But now—now it was surprising dozens of gentlemen weren't trailing after her, seeing to her every wish.

Quintin strode toward the back of the room and made his way over to where Lady Esther sat with her parents. A bit behind her and several strides to her left, he paused. What was he to say? She'd all but cast him off last time they had spoken. How was he to breach such a wall now? So many people were about, all sitting close by. It was hardly the place for a quiet, personal conversation.

Perhaps he should leave and find a different time to speak with her.

No, absolutely not. It had been days and he wasn't about to let this opportunity pass him up. From the row just behind Esther, a man and lady stood, moving down the aisle and toward the punch bowls in the back of the room. Quintin, not giving his doubts time to tell him otherwise, slipped down the same aisle and sat himself directly behind Esther. The awareness of her, no more than an arm's length away, made his whole body hum. Devil hang him—if ever he had wondered if he was wholly taken by Lady Esther, these past couple of weeks in London had most certainly proven he was.

Now he was here. And she was here. And they were quite close enough for conversation. What was he to say? She seemed unaware of his presence. He leaned forward. Hesitated. Sat back. If only they were on easy speaking terms once more. He would comment on the performance. She would say something she knew of the young lady—how hard she worked or that her family was well thought of in town. On and on they would go.

If only.

Opening and closing his fists, Quintin leaned forward once more. They were never going to be back to their old selves if he sat there mute.

"She seems quite accomplished."

Esther didn't jump at his voice, didn't so much as give a small start. Had she noticed him then? Been as aware of him as he was of her? Perhaps all was not lost.

"I understand," Esther angled her chin slightly toward him, but didn't look fully around, "that Lady Christina Enfield spends nearly two hours a day practicing."

Quintin could appreciate taking so much time for an endeavor that one saw as important. "It shows."

The corner of Esther's lips ticked up, but she didn't respond.

Quintin waited a minute. He probably should wait until the performances were over before speaking more with Esther, but he'd waited days to see her. "I heard about the mishap which befell your lady's maid."

"I did not know that had made its way into the rumor mill."

"Everyone is saying you were quite noble, staying with your maid until she was freed once more."

The small bit of smile left Esther's face. "Is that so?"

What had he said? Had the rumors been incorrect. Only, the story he'd heard sounded just like the kind of thing Esther would do. He'd had no cause to question it. What he *was* questioning was how to get her to smile once more. "I'm not surprised you insisted she be seen by a doctor. You've always been considerate."

Esther leaned ever so slightly away from him and faced the stage once more. Though Quintin wasn't fully sure, he *thought* she whispered, "Not always."

What did she mean by that? He couldn't think of a single person more considerate than Esther. He leaned in, wanting to ask her, but Esther pulled further away, speaking with a woman to her right.

Quintin sat back in his seat. Giving her space was part of his far-too-undefined plan. He didn't hear any of the rest of Lady Christina's performance. He didn't hear the next three either. Esther was too busy whispering to the women about her for him to speak with her anymore. Perhaps he should wait until all the performances were over. Then try and catch her before she left?

No. He'd been to these things before. The crush which was now contained in seats would be unleashed after the last bow was made. He glanced around the room, catching more than one gentleman glancing Esther's way. Apparently, he wasn't the only man hoping to speak with her tonight. He couldn't let her leave without having his say, though, and at least now she was somewhat trapped by the chairs and music.

He waited until she leaned away from the woman she had been whispering with. That conversation done, Quintin took hold of the opportunity before she started up another.

Quintin leaned forward. "Please tell me what's troubling you."

He sensed as much as saw her back stiffen. "Who says I'm troubled?" Her words said she wasn't, but her slightly strangled tone said she was.

"You know you can talk to me. You've always—"

"I am quite fine, Quintin." There was an edge to her words he'd never heard come from her before.

All right, then; if it was space she wanted, he wouldn't press the point. "At least tell me that we are still friends."

He expected her to smile, to say he was being a coxcomb for thinking they weren't. Instead, her lip trembled.

Quintin stifled a sigh. He was making far more of a mull of this whole situation than he had ever dreamed he would.

"Of course we're still friends," she said, her voice catching.

Were they? Everything about her tone and actions seemed to go against that statement. "Then why do you keep avoiding me?"

She didn't answer, but her hands began twisting in her lap. It brought to mind the many times he'd seen her trying her best to sit still during sermons, and only succeeding because their local vicar was a man of few words.

"I promise," Quintin spoke on, since Esther seemed disinclined to, "to respect your wishes. I won't call on you. I won't stand up with you more than once per ball"—though it killed him to say as much—"only please stop trying to avoid me. Tell me that I'm still free to speak with you when we're in company together?" He hoped that would be enough space. He hoped that, given a bit of time, she would remember that she could trust him. Maybe even tell him what was truly troubling her, for he knew something was.

"All right," she said.

He felt like jumping for joy. It wasn't the reception he'd originally hoped for when he first came to London, but after the past few days it felt like he'd scaled Mount Olympus. It was a good thing no one was looking at him just now; he was struggling to hide a wide smile.

"Actually," Esther said, leaning back and turning her chin toward him once more. "I believe I could use your assistance with something."

"Oh?" He leaned in closer. Not as close as he wanted to be to her, but still closer than he had been.

"Meet me tomorrow at Bloomstale's?"

The local haberdashery? "When?"

"In the afternoon, a little before supper."

"This sounds like the beginning of a fine adventure."

Her small smile slowly came back. Finally. "I believe it shall be."

CHAPTER 9

he cold days of winter seemed to be finally behind them. The touch of excitement which filled the air—a promise of summer just around the bend—reached into Quintin's chest and filled him with the desire to leap and shout. Spring was on its way. He loved this time of the year, when all the world was full of promise. When all the world was busy laying the foundation of a busy summer and a full harvest.

Moreover, Esther wanted his help with something. Some grand adventure. What could be better than that? There'd never been a better day for it either.

Quintin, in only a light jacket instead of his heavy greatcoat, dismounted and pushed into Bloomstale's. He was a touch early, nonetheless, Esther was already there. She stood near a selection of yellow ribbons, rubbing one the color of morning primrose between her finger and thumb. He hurried up beside her. He'd been unable to focus all morning. He'd racked his brain trying to figure out what Esther may be planning, but for the life of him he couldn't make heads nor tales of it.

"Good evening, Lady Esther," he said. Quintin still couldn't force himself to think of her as *Lady* Esther, but he knew such was required when they were out in society.

"Good evening, Lord Quintin."

He didn't like the sound of his title coming from her mouth, though the word didn't seem to stick against her lips as saying "Lady" had for him. It seemed she truly had moved on.

Unease slithering through him, he decided to keep the conversation light for a moment longer. "Did you enjoy the musicale last night?"

"Oh, yes. All the music was really quite lovely."

"Though none of it was as lovely as your watercolors. But I suppose one cannot exhibit such a talent at a musicale. You know," he said, unable to keep their conversation as impersonal as society expected any longer, "I have yet to see your paintings of India. Don't try to deny making any, either. I know you too well."

She didn't seem as happy at him bringing up her watercoloring as he'd expected. "I did a few," she said simply, not meeting his eyes. "When we first arrived."

That was it? That was all she was going to say on the subject? Esther loved her watercolors. "Will I be permitted to see them?"

"Perhaps someday." She half turned away from him, picking up a slip of ribbon and appearing to examine it.

Strange. Esther was suddenly acting quite like she had when he'd first arrived in London. He'd approached her and Lord Copeland and, though she'd been smiling at the time, he could tell by her eyes that something was wrong. She had the same look in her eyes now.

"Esther." He kept his voice low enough that no one else in the store would overhear. "Are you quite all right?"

"Of course." She turned sharply toward him, a blatantly forced smile on her lips. "Why would I not be? You know, you've rather surprised me, Lord Quintin."

Gads, but he hated her calling him by his formal name.

"We have been talking for well on a quarter of an hour and you have not once brought up our reason for meeting at all."

It was a clear change of topic. But ... well, if she wasn't ready to talk about what was bothering her, he felt it only kind to go along with what she *was* comfortable discussing.

"You are right. However, I must admit I have tried, and I cannot begin to guess at your adventure for the day."

Her face lit up. It wasn't her radiant smile, nor even her peaceful one. But something in between—something filled with spunk and determination. Whatever was bothering her, it seemed momentarily forgotten, and he was glad for it.

"Well," Esther said, her unhidden enthusiasm seeping from her tone. "I'll start by saying that if all goes well, it most certainly will take longer than just today."

"Interesting."

Esther turned away from the yellow ribbon and moved slowly closer to the shop front window. "Do you see my lady's maid, just there?" She nodded toward the small carriage sitting outside. A young woman sat in the back, and a driver hunched forward and clearly bored, sat in the front.

"The lady of the great stable loft escape?"

Esther laughed lightly. "The one and the same."

She was ever the only one who didn't mock his fanciful nature. "Are we here to buy flowers for her hair? Or should we just throw them at her feet?"

Esther lifted an eyebrow in question.

Quintin shrugged. "Don't all heroines get flowers in some manner at the end of the story?"

Esther leaned in, her voice dropping. "Ah, but what if I told you her story wasn't over yet?"

At her unexpected nearness, Quintin's heart sped up until it was nearly painful. He glanced away and over his shoulder, away from both the lady in the carriage and the lady at his side. He wasn't going to let anything ruin today, not even his own heart.

"You see," Esther continued, "the gossip about town is lacking one very important part of the story."

Quintin ground his jaw to keep his mind clear and returned to gazing out the window with Esther. "And what was that?" At least his voice was steady.

"That Joan there, has not stopped thinking about the handsome man who saved her ever since the incident."

"Ho-oh, is that so?"

Esther gave a satisfied nod and turned from the window. "The man is one of Lord Dunn's grooms, who also acts as a driver from time to time."

"Do you know the man's name?" Quintin could guess what Esther was thinking and that would require finding this manservant.

"He said it was Will Stanley."

"I only know *of* Lord Dunn. I've seen him a few times at White's since coming to London." Truth was, Quintin had heard rumors that, as a young earl, Dunn's estate had also struggled greatly. Quintin had debated asking the man for advice. But he didn't know much of the elderly man's character; would his questions be welcomed? "I've never had cause to notice his driver though. Will, you say his name is?"

"Yes, and if I didn't misunderstand the small look that passed between Will and Joan, I'd say he isn't likely to forget her, either."

"Isn't she a bit young for such things?" he asked.

"Not so young as to make it improper or even unusual. My last abigail married at her age."

"So we are, in fact, matchmaking?"

"Don't say it like that." Esther turned away from him and ran her fingers across folded sheets of fabric.

"Like what?"

"Like matchmaking is such a deplorable adventure. It's not, you know. Think of all the best stories; there's always a match in the end."

"I don't believe that story where the young boys protect their sister from an angry bear had any matches in the end."

She listed her head. "What story do you mean?"

"The one my father used to tell us when my brothers and I

couldn't quite get along." He didn't have many memories of the year after his mother died, and before Father remarried. But even his very young mind had held onto the feeling of loss that had seeped into their home; the memory of Father's stories had seemed like the only light in the darkness. Something had lifted in his chest whenever Father had told of heroes and grand ventures. The love of stories had seeped deep into him with each and every tale.

Esther shook her head and hit him lightly with a gloved hand. "That hardly counts." The feel of her hand against his arm, even in jest—no, especially in jest—was so like all those times they'd shared growing up. It was right; so very right.

"You were all much too young, I am sure," she continued, "for *real* tales."

"Real tales?"

"The kind with love and romance. Any tale without such things is quite lacking, I assure you."

"Is that so?"

"Yes. If you were older, no doubt, your father would have told you the *entire* tale, which included the young girl growing up to marry a prince and the boys becoming men and being wed to their heart's desire."

Quintin tried to push away the bite her statement brought. She wouldn't have known that in the story, Cassandra was the little girl and the brothers were Felix, Sheldon, and himself. Cassandra had, in fact, now married her prince. Felix and Sheldon, too, were wed to their heart's desire. Quintin was the only one who hadn't found his happy ending, it would seem.

"Well, if that's the case," he hurried on, wanting nothing more than to redirect the conversation away from himself, "then it's a very good thing that Joan, she of the stable loft caper, has a story which is not yet over."

Esther's hands came together in front of her, though she didn't fully hold still. Esther never did. Instead she stood *mostly* still but continued to twist side to side ever so slightly, just enough that her skirt swished about her softly. "I do truly believe she likes him. It's hardly surprising after the way they were thrown together. Do you not think it would be a grand thing if they *happened* to cross paths a few more times, just to see if he perhaps prefers her, too?" She looked up at him, all faux innocence.

His heart gave a jolt at the look and he couldn't stop a smile.

"Excellent," Esther crowed. She turned away and began fingering strips of cream-colored lace. His Esther—ever on the move. "Of course, if neither of them show a preference we will abandon the endeavor immediately. Only, I want to see if *maybe* they could find an understanding."

This was the Esther he'd fallen in love with ever so many years ago. The woman who laughed and teased and was concerned for others. Someone who couldn't remain still for the love of life, packed inside her very self.

"Sounds like a diverting adventure," he said. Though, the word "diverting" felt nowhere near a strong enough term.

Esther moved up beside him and slipped her arm through his. This time it was her exuberant smile which lighted her face. "Then come; let us discuss the best way to proceed."

CHAPTER 10

*H*yde Park was not nearly so full today as Esther expected it would be in two months' time, when the Season was in full swing. Still, there was quite the gathering today. As a young woman, she'd often daydreamed of taking a ride at the fashionable hour through Hyde Park. Even the thought had given her chills of excitement. Today was ever so much more than she'd imagined. Not only was it thrilling to be out on a warm day with so many other people also enjoying spring, but she and Quintin had their own secret adventure they were embarking on.

"It seems winter has made its last stand," Esther said, sitting in the forward-facing seat of Quintin's carriage. Joan sat quietly beside her. Normally Esther would have been miffed by Mother's insistence that her abigail accompany them on this outing. But this time, Mother's ridiculous prejudice against Quintin had played in their favor.

"None too soon, either," Quintin said. He sat in the rear-facing seat, making room for Joan. He was well turned out today, in a smart top hat, a perfectly shaped cravat, and polished Hessians. For a man who didn't care much for impressing others, he certainly had a good eye for fashion.

"I cannot say I'll miss the cold. Snow may be nice on Twelfth Night, but now that the holidays are over, I'm ready for the warmth of spring." It felt odd talking of something as inane as the weather with Quintin. Yet, with Joan sitting directly beside her, they couldn't talk of their actual intentions just now. Still, Esther was getting quite sick of speaking of the weather. Sometimes she wondered if anyone among the *ton* could go a full day *without* commenting on what was obvious to anyone who looked out a window.

Quintin didn't look at her when he responded with, "Quite right." Instead, he scanned both the carriages which passed them and the ones which lingered behind them.

"Do tell me," she said, breaking through the few minutes of silence. "Have you spoken to anyone about Cottonhold yet?"

His mouth worked back and forth for a moment. "Not precisely," he said slowly.

She didn't respond, but also pinned him with enough of a stare that he would know better than to change the topic.

Quintin leaned forward, resting his arms against his knees. "You know me. I've never been one to talk on and on about myself."

"You don't have to be." She would never ask him to change who he was. "Only, I think it would be beneficial if you spoke with a man or two who has been where you are."

"If I knew such a man and I knew he was willing to help, I'd have no problem asking."

"You should approach Lord Durham or Lord Briston. Or even Lord Dunn. They've all had estate problems in the past and in the times they've visited Father, they were all quite congenial."

"To a beautiful woman, no doubt they were."

She pursed her lips. "It wasn't anything like that. I truly think they would be willing to help if only you asked."

Quintin seemed ready to argue further, but something behind her must have caught his eye, for he paused then leaned back in his seat once more. Tapping their driver on the back, he whispered to the man to slow down slightly. Their carriage driver did so immediately.

Esther resisted the strong urge to turn around and see if it was, in fact, Lord Dunn behind them. It had to be. The whole point of this trip to Hyde Park was to try and find him. Esther had heard rumors that the longstanding bachelor was finally courting a woman, a widow of substantial means.

A large barouche pulled up beside theirs. Esther didn't recognize the gray-haired man or the middle-aged woman beside him. But she most certainly recognized the young man driving the elaborate carriage. Will Stanley. She also didn't miss Joan's small intake of breath as they pulled up beside Quintin's carriage.

"Good day to you, sir," Quintin called.

"Good day. Yes, a good day to you too, Lord Quintin." Lord Dunn seemed in high spirits at the moment. Was he typically that way, or was it simply the smiling woman beside him?

Quintin asked a question—something about Lord Dunn's newest horse—and then simply sat back and let the man go. Apparently, Quintin had perfected the art of remaining quiet while out in society. That single question led to Lord Dunn speaking for a full ten minutes, barely pausing to draw breath. All Quintin had to do after that first question was nod here and there, or hum approvingly.

It was too bad they weren't in a place where Quintin could ask questions regarding how to better run an estate. Perhaps if she kept at it, Quintin would see that most men would not think less of him for knowing his estate was struggling. Many men faced such a dilemma. Esther herself certainly felt no less for him because of his current situation.

Esther pretended to be interested in the horse's breeding and temperament. The problem certainly wasn't that she disliked horses; she liked them quite a lot. But she was perfectly situated, seated as she was directly beside Joan, to catch the several glances Will was throwing the abigail over his shoulder.

Satisfaction swelled up inside Esther; she'd been certain something had begun between the two. Quintin had quietly looked into the man as well and learned that he was known for being a hard worker, for his loyalty to Lord Dunn, and for treating the maids of the house with respect. He seemed the perfect man for Joan.

"And how are you enjoying London so far, Lady Esther?"

The widow's question caught Esther off guard and she very nearly started in her seat.

"Quite well, I assure you."

"Well, of course," the widow continued, her voice deeper than Esther would have expected, but she seemed kind, "how could one not when with such company?" Her eyes returned to Lord Dunn and she smiled.

With a look like that in her eyes, Esther was quite certain that Will and all his fellow servants would soon be celebrating their master's wedding.

After a polite farewell, Lord Dunn's carriage moved on. Though Will and Joan were not able to speak to one another during the exchange, it had been clear to Esther that they both had wanted to. She shared a knowing, confident smile with Quintin. This was good. This had been a subtle step toward their end goal. Such things were always necessary when adventuring. Push too hard at the beginning and one was liable to take a misstep.

"Lord Quintin, what an unexpected pleasure."

Esther glanced over. Where Lord Dunn's barouche had once been was now a small equipage. Lady Christina, the same woman who'd played at Garrison's musicale a few nights before sat inside, her mother beside her.

"Lady Christina," Quintin said, inclining his head.

"Good day, Lady Esther," Christina's mother said.

Christina didn't so much as glance Esther's way, her eyes staying on Quintin. "Mother and I could not bear to be indoors any longer. We have been enjoying a most lovely day, too."

Quintin did no more than nod, and on Lady Christina went. "Have you ever seen such a pleasant day? I actually heard birds this morning when I awoke. Fancy that. Birds. I mean, we hear them often enough at our country estate, but here in Town it is a far more rare occurrence."

Quintin continued to nod, and Lady Christina continued to talk. Esther knew very little about Lady Christina; she'd heard that the woman was well liked by most and that she was quite dedicated in her practice at the pianoforte.

Esther shifted about in the carriage, then shifted again. She glanced away from Lady Christina, eying the large oak tree not far off instead. It would be grand to stretch her legs just now and walk instead of ride.

Esther suddenly wished someone had thought to warn her that the woman didn't need any help to carry a conversation. But then, she hardly could have done anything to stop Lady Christina from greeting them. Esther listened tiredly as the lady moved on, hardly taking a breath, from birds to the new dress she was having made and how it made her feel quite elegant, then to the opera she'd attended the previous night and how she hadn't thought the soprano did the audience any favors.

Esther twisted her lips to the side. It was truly unfortunate that a lady exiting a carriage halfway through Hyde Park just to stretch her legs was far from acceptable. *Finally*, Lady Christina's mother bid them good afternoon and off they rode.

Esther appreciated the silence the moment they left. "You know," she said to Quintin after they, too, had begun to roll along the pavement, "she wouldn't go on so if you only spoke up now and then."

"When? I didn't know one could squeeze so many words into so few breaths."

Esther allowed him a bit of silence on the journey back home. After that, he would want it. Once back in front of Whinston House, Quintin stepped down and then handed out first Esther, and then Joan.

Esther slowed her step, allowing Joan plenty of time to enter her family's London house. Glancing about, Esther found no one too nearby.

She reached out and took Quintin's arm, speaking softly. "I feel that went quite well, do you not?"

"I think you have the right of it," he whispered back, leaning in closer. "They have indeed caught one another's eye."

"Now, the only problem is we need to find a means for them to talk with one another."

"Yes, glancing at one another from separate carriages is hardly enough."

"Thoughts?"

"I know Lord Dunn visits White's often."

She threw him a flat stare. "Truly, Quintin? I cannot be seen visiting White's with or without my abigail."

He chuckled low. He'd always laughed with her easily, though his laugh was far deeper now. It was a subtle reminder that they weren't children any longer, neither of them. It left her feeling a touch nostalgic but also drew out a different feeling all together—something heady which sent her heart beating. She blinked, and it was quite suddenly as though she were seeing him for the first time all over again. Only, not as a boy, such as they'd originally met. But as a man. Tall, sandy hair, vivid blue eyes. Drat—he was so handsome. Why did he have to grow into such a handsome man? Keeping her distance would have been imminently easier if he'd grown up to be bland.

Slowly he took one step closer to her and then another. Esther tried to draw in a cooling breath. With him so close, she needed a fan or, at the very least, a cool breeze.

"Well," he asked, "where *do* you take your abigail?"

Will and Joan. They were talking about *Will and Joan*. She needed to focus. "Not nearly so many places as Lord Dunn might take his driver." Hopefully her voice sounded wholly unaffected. Oh, how she'd wished for a moment just like this countless times while in India. Moments when they were together, talking, standing beside one another. Only, such nearness was proving far more alluring than she'd ever imagined. Even in those moments when she'd allowed her mind free rein, she'd failed to include the heat across her skin and the way she was suddenly aware of every inch of herself.

"She's always here though, is she not?" he asked.

An idea sparked through her brainbox. "Quintin, that's perfect. We'll get Lord Dunn to bring Will *here* again." This is why she told Quintin of her plans; he always understood and helped. "My coming-out ball is next week. I'll make sure Mother has included Lord Dunn on the guest list." That would be just the thing. If Lord Dunn had Will drive him to the ball, he and Joan would have plenty of time to talk. Exuberance veritably pulsed through her. Oh, it was perfect. Going up on tiptoe, Esther threw her arms around Quintin, hugging him tightly. She'd certainly hugged him before, when they were children. But this time, the moment her arms wrapped around him, she was once more aware that they were children no longer. She was a grown woman, hugging a grown man with whom she had no understanding.

What had she been thinking? It had been the thrill of the moment, the closeness they'd shared in making plans together.

Quintin was not returning her hug; he hadn't lost his head to thoughts of Will and Joan as she so quickly had. As Esther pulled back, Quintin tipped his head her direction, their noses barely brushing against one another.

"Thank you for helping me help Joan," she said, voice trembling. What were the chances that he'd be as anxious to brush off her sudden foolishness as she?

One of his arms came up and circled around her waist, keeping her from stepping away. "I will always be willing to help you, Esther. No matter what goes wrong for you, I'll always be someone you can count on."

A tingling ripple of fear whispered that he'd found out—that he knew the truth of India and all she'd done. Esther took a large step back, breaking free of him. The air about her felt cold. Had she truly wished for a breeze only moments ago? She felt near to shivering now.

"Thank you," she said as nonchalantly as she could manage,

even while folding her arms tightly to her chest. "I'm glad to have you help me with this," she said, though part of her brain insisted that when Quintin had said he'd always be someone she could count on, he hadn't been talking of Will and Joan.

"Well, I suppose I should be off," Quintin said. His voice sounded strange. So many emotions seemed to be trapped just behind his words, too many for even her to tease apart. Sadness perhaps, possibly even regret. Hope maybe? "Will you be at the Monstattens' supper party tomorrow?"

At least he wasn't demanding they talk about her flying at him like a girl still in pigtails. "I do not know if my mother has decided our plans for tomorrow evening or not." She could almost see him draw into himself. The subtle way he leaned back, the infinitesimal stiffening around his jaw. She'd so much enjoyed today—with no talk of futures or pasts—and didn't want to ruin it now. A desperate need to keep him close rose up in her. "I will speak with her and see if I can't convince her the Monstattens' gathering is the best choice."

"It's only supper, some cards, and maybe a song or two." He glanced past her, down the empty street. He seemed to be already bracing himself for her blatant, if polite, rejection. "I know your mother prefers large crushes."

But she didn't want to reject him. She didn't want to lose him. Not completely. They'd reached some kind of comfortable friendship today and Esther wasn't willing to let her moment of childish stupidity ruin it all. "I *will* speak to my mother and get her to agree to going to Monstattens'. I promise."

CHAPTER 11

Quintin's eyes moved down the long line of numbers. Costs were up. Savings were down. His brain seemed unable to calculate anything more specific than that.

Leaning back heavily in his chair, he stared across the room at the crackling fire. Shelves lined with books filled either side of the hearth. He missed Cottonhold. Here, at Ramport House, the shelves held history books and philosophy books and a few books on mathematics. The one thing the books all had in common was the author approached their individual subject with an air of superiority, many dates and facts, and no story at all.

Back at Cottonhold, however, Quintin had used what small funds he had at his disposal and filled nearly every shelf with books he found most diverting. They included poetry and mythology, even a few novels. Though he didn't care for the more lurid stories, he had found several novels which he'd struggled to put down. Those ones had, consequently, found a permanent home on his shelves.

Quintin looked back at his ledger. Books were all he was going to afford for the next several decades if he couldn't get his affairs in order. Quintin, alone in the room, let out a loud growl and settled further into the chair. Tipping his head back and resting it against the top of his chair, he closed his eyes.

Esther immediately came to view. The corner of his mouth tipped up. Gads, but he'd had fun with her yesterday in Hyde Park. Though they'd both grown, it was so easy to slip back into who they'd been. Best friends. Chief allies. Each other's favorite accomplice.

Then she'd hugged him.

Quite suddenly, *quite* unexpectedly.

The moment washed over him. Nothing had prepared him for how perfectly she had felt against him. He'd wanted more than anything to wrap his arms around her and keep her there for time unmeasured. But doing so would have been a mistake. Life, it would seem, had divined to serve him a sobering paradox. For, in pulling Esther close, he no doubt would have driven her away. Even placing one arm around her back seemed almost too much. She'd put distance between them immediately and had clearly wanted to forget the incident.

That bit of truth was like a knife to the gut.

Esther had hugged him during the excitement of the moment and the instant she'd realized what she'd been doing, she'd stopped and wished it undone.

Hang it all, what was he to do? Her friendship was more important to him than any he'd ever known. Yet, he wanted more. And she clearly did not.

A knock sounded at the door. Quintin sat upright, the chair squeaking at the sudden movement. "Come."

The butler opened the door and bowed. "My lord, there is a John Willoughby and Henry Coleston to see you."

Blast. This was bound to be bad news. "Have them shown in here." The butler bowed again and left. Quintin steepled his fingers atop the desk and leaned forward. That his man of business had come was not too big of a surprise. That the farmer who saw to

Quintin's most northern spot of land had also come all the way to London was far more unnerving. Footsteps echoed from the hallway past the door. Well, it wasn't as though he'd have to wait long.

The door opened and the two men were waved inside. John pushed his way in, clearly comfortable walking about the London home of a marquess. Henry Coleston, however, all but tiptoed in. Hat in his hands, he glanced all about the room as he moved toward the desk where Quintin sat. He looked as though he believed hidden birds of prey were magically sewn into the wall-paper and, at any moment, would fly from the walls and extract what little coin the man had on his person as payment for entering the room.

"Lord Quintin," John began without preamble. "I am afraid we bring bad news."

He'd feared as much. "Please, be seated." He pointed toward the two chairs facing the desk. John sat promptly, while Henry eyed the chair instead. "It's all right, Henry. You are my guest." No doubt, the man, who had previously been merely an assistant gardener before Quintin's father had granted him a bit of land to farm, keenly felt out of place in such a grand room.

Henry finally sat, but only on the very edge of the chair. Well, it was better than the man standing for the entirety of the visit.

"So tell me, John, what has gone wrong this time?"

John leaned back and motioned with his hand for Henry to speak.

Henry's face crumbled a bit, deep lines spreading from his eyes. "I beg your pardon, my lord, but it was last week. I'd planted a mite early, in the hopes of a better harvest. Then that late frost hit."

The news hit Quintin's stomach like a boulder. "How much was lost?" He didn't dare hope Henry would say "very little."

"Nearly all 'o it, my lord."

"Blast." Quintin cupped one hand over his eyes, blocking out the site of either man.

The room was silent for a bit. Finally, Quintin pulled his hand away. Henry was clearly miserable. Poor man. It wasn't his fault that the heavens had chosen to send a late frost. There was no way to predict that such would have taken place. If it hadn't, then the early planting would have been a much-needed boon. As it was, there weren't many options available.

"Have you the means to replant?" Quintin asked, though he knew his tenants well enough to know the answer.

"No, my lord."

Quintin shook his head, running a hand through his hair. Just once—just once!—he'd like to get through a season without one set back or another. Spring, summer, autumn, winter; not one had passed since he'd taken over Cottonhold without some catastrophe taking place.

Thoughts of "seasons" brought a whole different type of season to mind. The London Season. He was failing in that regard, too.

"Don't worry, Henry," Quintin said softly. "I'll see to it that new seed is bought and delivered to your farm." Any other time, he'd have ridden out and seen the farm himself before offering such help. But he couldn't leave London right now. Not with things so unsettled between him and Esther.

"Oh, my lord, that is very merciful."

"Think nothing of it." Though there was no doubt in Quintin's mind that he, himself, would be thinking of little else for the next while. How was he ever to afford first, feed for sheep and now, a field's worth of seed? But it had to be done. It was either that or Henry's family would starve come next winter.

Quintin excused Henry, knowing John would have something to say as well before leaving. As Henry moved out the door, Quintin called to the footman just outside.

"Show Henry to the parlor and have tea and biscuits brought."

"Yes, my lord," the footman said with a bow before closing the door once more.

Quintin looked at John. His man of business did not appear happy.

"Well?" he finally asked.

"You do realize," John started, "that as master of Cottonhold you have full legal rights to excuse any of the farmers you wish and replace them with better experienced men, right?"

"Of course I know, John."

"First Martin Soames and now Henry Coleston. My lord, you cannot continue to pay for every one of your farmers' lack of intelligence in this manner."

"And if I excuse Henry, what will become of him? What of his family?"

"The man was a good gardener. No doubt he can find such a position again."

"I cannot like such an idea, John. His daughters are nearing marrying age. Such a reversal in station would only harm their prospects."

John's features drooped, a clear indication that he thought a man's daughters' prospects should in no way interfere with Quintin's decision to keep said man on or not. Quintin shook his head and leaned back in his chair. John, nearing his forties, had probably forgotten what the marriage mart was like. Quintin couldn't forget, not when it stared him in the face every day.

"Take a look at the books," he said.

John's voice rose. "I've been looking at the books. We don't have the funds—"

"We do. We just need to find them." If nothing else, he'd ask his father for money. The thought made his insides twist. Father would help, but he would also think him a failure. Nearly anything would be better than that.

Nearly anything. If it was between showing his father exactly how inept he was at being master of Cottonhold or dismissing Henry, he'd choose speaking with his father.

"It'll be all right, John. You'll see. We aren't beat yet."

John harrumphed, most unconvinced.

Quintin folded his arms and deigned not to reply to John's wordless disagreement. "How are Martin's sheep?"

"The doctor arrives in a few days' time. The new feed seems to be helping somewhat; we've had fewer losses as of late. But it hasn't stemmed the problem entirely."

"Progress is progress."

"So long as it isn't too little, too late."

"It won't be. You'll see."

John leaned forward. "You need to return, sir. Cottonhold always runs smoother when you're present."

Not smooth enough, however. Quintin had been in residence at Cottonhold nearly every day for the past four years and it hadn't proven enough.

Either way, Esther was still here.

"I can't. Not yet."

"My lord, allow me to be frank."

"You know I always prefer that you are." Though he did wish the man was a little less of a harbinger. Quintin usually didn't mind John's dark stance, but today it was quickly ebbing away Quintin's hope.

"Whatever has brought you to London will be for naught if you do not see to Cottonhold first. No matter who she is, her father won't be charmed by a man whose estate is on the brink of collapse."

Quintin felt the jab, sharp and biting, in the pit of his stomach. "Thank you, John."

He stood. Continuing this meeting would be pointless. "I appreciate you bringing Henry all this way."

"My lor—"

"Good day, John."

John ground his jaw and rose as well. "I will get the details of seed costs from Henry, run the calculations, and let you know where you stand."

"Very well."

John moved to the door. With a hand on the knob, he glanced back at Quintin, but apparently decided against speaking anything more for he slipped from the room silently.

Quintin collapsed back into the chair. Stupid man. Stupid notion of whom Esther's father would or would not allow her to marry. Still, the pain in his stomach would not ease.

It wouldn't because, simply put, Quintin feared John was right.

CHAPTER 12

*C*onvincing Mother to attend the Monstattens' supper party instead of the opera turned out to be a much harder sell than Esther had originally assumed. Mother cared as little about what Esther wanted to do as she ever had. It was only after she subtly let it slip that Lord Copeland was rumored to have been included on the guest list that Mother had agreed.

Esther sat as still as she could muster while Joan pulled her hair up first one way and then another. Esther tried hard not to stare at her abigail. Did the woman know she and Quintin had only taken a turn about Hyde Park so she could see Will once more? Esther didn't think they'd been too obvious; it certainly wasn't something most members of the *ton* would do.

"Don't tilt your head so, my lady," Joan gently scolded.

Esther righted herself once more, the excitement simmering inside her escaping in the form of her hands twisting about each other instead.

"You are fidgeting even more than usual, my lady. Are you nervous for tonight?" Joan asked.

"No, more just excited." Though truthfully, her thoughts were not on tonight at all, but on Joan and Will.

"I'm glad to hear it," Joan said. "You've been so melancholy as of late, I'd begun to worry over you."

Esther's brow creased. Mother had said nearly those same words to her earlier that day. Even one of Mother's close friends, Lady Williamson, had said something similar last week. Esther didn't like the feeling that others might inadvertently learn of her horrid actions in India simply because she didn't feel like rattling on about the weather like other women sometimes did. Still, she should probably try to be more like herself.

"Did you enjoy our outing today?" Esther redirected the conversation. She wanted to come straight out and ask Joan if she had been surprised, possibly excited, to see Will again. But she wasn't altogether sure the young woman would appreciate Esther meddling in her affairs. A roundabout approach was best.

"Yes, my lady, I enjoyed it very much."

Esther wanted to twist around in her seat and face Joan, eye to eye, but she dutifully remained facing the mirror. "Enjoyed the spring air? Or enjoyed the company?"

Esther caught Joan's dropped brow through the mirror. "I'm sure Lord Quintin is a fine man, though it's not my place to say otherwise."

Esther's lips pursed. Lord Quintin wasn't who she had in mind at all. "Lord Quintin is quite the finest man in all London. However, I must say I was pleased to see Will again. We both owe him quite a debt of gratitude."

Joan pinked, but stayed silent.

"Come now, Joan." This time Esther did pull free of Joan's hands and turned fully in her seat. "You can tell me. Do you not think him quite a handsome man?"

"Oh, yes." Joan suddenly sighed, her hands dropping to her sides. "And clearly quite generous, or else he would not have come to my rescue so quickly." She walked around Esther, leaning a hip against the small vanity table. "I spoke to Cook about him. She heard from another maid in Lord Dunn's household that Will Stanley is in very high standings with his lordship. Rumors have it that Lord Dunn even recommended him to a duke. Can you imagine?" Her hands clasped tightly, she eyed the ceiling. "Working for a duke." She sighed again and then glanced back down at Esther. "He must be very good to be recommended for such an honor."

"There is no doubt of it in my mind," Esther said. "He seemed nothing short of entirely competent the few times I've had chance to meet him." She hoped a good man like Will would be hired on by a duke. Esther, though born of the upper echelon, was by no means blind to the fact that the higher the household, the higher the status *all* members of the household enjoyed.

"Furthermore," Esther continued, "I do believe you've caught his eye."

"Do you, miss? Truthfully?"

Esther patted Joan's clasped hands. "I wouldn't say so if I didn't believe it."

"I don't know much about such things."

"Well, neither of you knows the other full well, but I think it's safe to say he wishes that were not the case."

Joan moved about around Esther, picking up the last few unpinned locks and forcing Esther to look into the mirror once more. "I don't see how the situation would remedy itself. I haven't any cause to visit Dunn House and unless his lordship wishes to speak with your father, Will has no cause to visit here."

It was a dilemma. One that Esther had mulled over constantly for several days now. Granted, Lord Dunn would be attending her coming out ball, but perhaps there was some way Joan could happen across Will before then. "Could we not come up with some excuse for you to visit Dunn House?" She'd thought up several over the past few days, but none of which would hold water. She would hate for Joan to appear as though she were coming to call on Will. Imagine, a woman calling on a man? It was not to be borne. She'd be ridiculed for sure. And would no doubt catch the attention of all the wrong sorts of men.

"Oh, no," Joan said, her voice growing smaller. "I'm quite sure I could not."

"But suppose we had a very good reason? You could say you were fetching something for Mrs. White." Whinston House's housekeeper was quite often known to have had communication with members of other households. Though Esther couldn't say she knew exactly how or why such communications took place.

"Mrs. White has never had cause to speak with Miss Collier before."

"Who?"

"Lord Dunn's housekeeper."

Of course.

"Miss Collier is quite old and not overly fond of idle chatter. She'd question me for sure, if I showed up. Then she'd question Mrs. White. I'm sure to be found out." Her voice quaked slightly.

"Yes, it is quite a puzzlement."

"*Puzzlement*, my lady?"

"I read that word in the paper last week. Don't you find it just delicious?"

"If you say so. But it sounds a bit too high for the likes of me." Joan stepped back, away from Esther's chair and held up a second mirror so Esther could see all sides of her updo.

Esther twisted first one way and then the other. "Joan, you have outdone yourself." She lowered the mirror and smiled at her abigail. "Again."

"Thank you, my lady. It's not hard when I have someone as pretty as you to fix up." They quickly moved from hair to dressing Esther. Soon the process was done, and Joan left through the servants' door. Esther watched her slip out and then turned back toward the mirror. She supposed she looked well enough; she'd shared a happy and carefree expression with Joan, but she didn't quite feel so.

The memory of her arms around Quintin still hung close to her. Every time she closed her eyes she relived that brief, heavenly moment. Forcing her eyes away from the mirror, her gaze fell, unbidden, to the pile of untouched papers, brushes, and small jars of paints pushed to the back of her desk.

Quintin had asked about her watercolors of India. Slowly, she strode over and pulled out one of her many small notebooks. Perhaps she *should* pull out her paints once more. She certainly had much here in London she would love to try and capture in a picture.

She pulled the notebook open. It fell immediately to a half-finished painting of some of the ruins in India. Hot shame rushed off the page and leapt at her. Her eyes stung, and suddenly she felt it hard to breathe. The unexpected wave of unadulterated self-loathing caught her so off guard, she nearly collapsed onto the nearby chair.

Esther snapped the book shut. Setting her jaw, she shoved the book back to where she'd found it. No, she could never show those to Quintin. Blinking, she hurried back over to the mirror—she couldn't go tonight looking as though she'd been crying. The paleness of her own face surprised her. It had only been a book. Only an unfinished watercolor. It was stupid and childish to respond so. Esther pinched her cheeks, wishing there was a better way to draw color back into them.

Flatly refusing to glance over at her paints again, Esther moved toward the door. She hadn't painted since her encounter with the hateful Lieutenant Fallow. Moreover, if she couldn't find a way to keep some semblance of calm while looking at her own work, she may never be able to paint again. The realization almost made her cry, in truth. She had always *loved* her watercolors.

Her conversation with Joan from moments ago came back to her. It was true that puzzlement was a most delicious word. Unfortunately, it also quite adequately described her whole world right now.

CHAPTER 13

*E*sther stepped out of the carriage. The sun had long since set, but dozens of candles lighted the way to the Monstattens' front door. A cacophony of horses' hooves against stone and carriage wheels rattling mixed with the call of coachmen and grooms. Esther glanced about. She didn't see Will anywhere. It didn't matter anyway; it wasn't as though she'd brought Joan. One did not bring her own abigail to a simple supper party.

"Oh look, Lady Williamson is here," Mother, who'd exited the carriage just before her, said. Not allowing Esther time to respond, Mother hurried off to speak with her friend.

"Your mother truly did feel deprived of society while in India, didn't she?"

Esther smiled at Quintin's voice, but didn't turn around. "She felt it far more keenly than I did."

She felt him move up closer from behind. "Did you not miss much of England then?"

She'd missed him. Oh gracious, how she'd missed him. "A few things."

"Tell me," he whispered.

Esther turned around. He was so close. Esther clasped her

hands together behind her back. The small slip of air between them shivered with awareness. He was well turned out tonight. She hadn't expected anything less. "I missed . . ." She tried to formulate a coherent thought. Something that didn't reveal too much of the truth. He was so close, yet all she wanted was for him to be closer still. The soft candlelight flickering around them seemed to block out the rest of the world. It was as though only he and she existed, two lone individuals in a world of darkness. She'd not forgotten the feel of throwing her arms around him yesterday. The more she thought back on the incident the more one emotion pulsed inside her: longing.

She'd dreamed so many times of being in Quintin's arms—not as school children holding on to each other to keep from falling off the log and into the river—but as adults, holding on to each other out of love.

She leaned in slightly, and Quintin responded in kind. He smelled good. She couldn't remember ever thinking that of him before. It seemed not *all* was as it had been.

"You missed?" he prompted.

Right. She was supposed to be telling him what she missed while away in India, not letting her mind wander to forbidden thoughts of him and her and being in his arms.

"I missed ... cool breezes."

"Cool breezes?" He chuckled softly. His laugh was so much deeper than when they were young. She'd always enjoyed laughing with him in the past, but it had always been the act of being *able* to laugh together that she'd enjoyed. Now, she not only appreciated that she could be herself around him, but she found the sound of his laugh was quickly becoming one of her favorite things to hear.

"Yes, it was quite hot in India."

"I've heard such is to be expected. Though I can't say I know from experience."

"You always said you were going to travel the entire continent someday," Esther said. "Why haven't you?"

A bit of his smile fell away. "I'm afraid the opportunity has yet to present itself."

"Yet to present itself?" That didn't sound like her Quintin. He had a propensity toward being quiet, but that certainly didn't translate into a propensity to sit about doing nothing. "I've never known you to wait on Opportunity. I thought you believed in going out and getting it yourself." It wasn't as though, as third son of a marquess, Quintin lacked the means to travel.

His brow creased. "Yes, well . . ."

"Cottonhold?"

"Precisely. But," he brought a finger up, "before you go on again about me speaking to other gentlemen, I'll have you know that I have."

"Truly?"

"Don't act so surprised," he said with a wink. "And yes, I spoke with Lord Briston like you recommended. Furthermore, I wrote to Lord Dunn this morning and he's agreed to meet with me in two days' time."

"Excellent. Did Lord Briston have any suggestions? Anything you feel might help?"

"Yes, actually. We spoke at some length. He's recommended a sheep doctor and—"

"Lady Esther." A third voice broke into their temporarily isolated world.

She turned and found Lord Copeland striding her way. Though he smiled, there was a tightness about his mouth which made him seem less than fully at ease. The bit of light from the house made the tip of his nose seem more bulbous than usual, though noticing as such, even to herself, was quite unkind. Esther chided herself silently.

"Good evening, Lord Quintin," he said.

"Copeland," was Quintin's stiff reply.

Lord Copeland extended his elbow toward Esther. "Allow me the pleasure of escorting you inside, my lady."

There was no polite way to refuse him; though she was loath to leave Quintin and quit their short tête-à-tête. The moment her hand touched Lord Copeland's arm, he tugged her a few feet away. She got the distinct impression he was not so much pulling her toward himself as Lord Copeland was pulling her *away* from Quintin.

"Bad luck, I'm afraid, old chap," Lord Copeland said to Quintin. Though his words were cheerful, there was an edge to his tone. "You've delayed asking to see Lady Esther inside too long and now have lost out entirely."

Quintin smiled back, quite as if not a word of what Lord Copeland had said bothered him. But it did. Esther could see it in his eyes. She knew those eyes too well to miss it.

"So it would seem," Quintin said.

Not allowing him time to say more, Lord Copeland turned them around and led Esther into the Monstattens' supper party.

QUINTIN JOINED THE MONSTATTENS' PARLOR A FEW MINUTES AFTER Esther had entered on Lord Copeland's arm. She hadn't missed Mother's triumphant smile when they had, nor did she miss Lady Christina's constant presence near Quintin's side.

Supper was no less pleasant. She was seated with Lord Copeland on one side, and a Lord Elles—a "very eligible gentleman" as Mother had put it in a hurried whisper when they were being seated—on the other. Mother herself was directly across the way. She felt pinned down by the three. Not a moment was left to silence. Lord Elles asked about her trip to India; Esther replied with a proper remark on the weather. Lord Copeland brought up the spices he'd heard tales of; Esther toned down her reply, wishing she was talking to Quintin instead, and responded that the curries she'd tried were quite different than anything she'd had in England. Mother mentioned several of the more prestigious individuals they'd "dined with often and freely" while in India. Both lords acted appropriately impressed, which led Mother to smile all the more.

Esther stole as many glances down the table as she dared. Lady Christina was sitting beside Quintin. Esther kept her huff silent. Of course that woman would have found a way to sit beside *her* Quintin. Why did Lady Christina suddenly have such a penchant for him? He wasn't at all the type of man whom she'd see the woman wanting to be with. She hazarded another glance.

Quintin was sitting silently, nodding as Lady Christina spoke.

No, she was wrong. Quintin was precisely the sort of man a woman like that would want. Silent. Willing to listen. He wouldn't interrupt. He would never tell her that talk of ribbons or society columns or anything else she spoke on was inane or beneath him. It was too bad Lord Copeland couldn't be a bit more like that. Only two days ago, she'd begun speaking on how much she enjoyed climbing trees as a girl, and his only response was to clearly state that such was a pointless activity, especially for a female.

An aching pulsed from Esther's chest. Quintin would have listened. He would have heard all she had to say and then replied kindly. He would have agreed that climbing trees was just the sort of thing a child—boy or girl—should do. Then, he would have told her that she truly looked lovely in evening primrose. He would have said that she should not worry about the gossipmongers and counseled her to keep her head up. All those little bits of encouragement she'd grown quite used to when they were young.

The thought of him directing such attentions to another woman stung, biting hard and sharp.

The pain did not lessen as supper was concluded and the ladies withdrew back to the parlor. Mother was directly by Esther's side as they sat not far from the hearth, a glowing fire therein. At least both Lord Copeland and Lord Elles were still in the dining room with their port. That at least provided some reprieve.

Conversation flowed around Esther, but for the first time in as long as she could remember, Esther didn't feel like joining in. Lady Williamson sat beside Mother and the two began speaking in hurried tones. Someone across the room asked Lady Christina to play and, after consenting, she sat at the pianoforte. Lady

Williamson leaned over, speaking around Mother and to Esther directly.

"Lord Copeland looks quite well turned out tonight, does he not?"

Not as well as Quintin. "Yes, he does."

Lady Williamson and Mother shared a look. "He is the earl of a sizable estate, I understand?"

"Yes," Esther replied again, not at all wishing to continue discussing Lord Copeland. "I believe he is."

Another shared look.

"Well, well," Lady Williamson said, leaning back once more. "Isn't that nice."

Was all of London speaking of herself and Lord Copeland in such a way? Esther certainly hoped not.

The men joined them a few minutes later. Lords Copeland and Elles sat in a couple of chairs to Esther's right. They spoke of first this mutual acquaintance, and then that one. The room soon filled with the buzz of conversation. Through it all, Esther could easily pick out the tones of Lady Christina at the pianoforte, Quintin once again beside her.

"I do hope Lord Featherstone will sell me his prize mare's newest colt," Lord Copeland said.

Esther nodded; she needed to stay focused on the conversation in which she was expected to participate. "Yes, that would be quite nice, I am sure."

Lord Copeland smiled at her agreement and continued on about the new colt. Esther tried her best to stay focused on his words, but each word seemed to slip away just as soon as she tried to reel the next one in. She'd always suspected that Quintin could—and often preferred—to listen to the conversations around him with half his brain, reserving the other half for more adventuresome thoughts. He'd once confided in her that he'd had glorious ideas of how they could defeat the "unholy banshee of Withering Grove" while listening to that Sunday's sermon. At first, she'd thought little of it; she, too, had spent all the sermon thinking of their imaginary foe.

However, when she'd pressed Quintin, she'd found he not only had come up with grand ideas, he'd also remembered the sermon almost word for word.

Another time, they'd been pinned down by her mother and forced to sit with her and her friend during an at-home. Those fifteen minutes had felt like an eternity to Esther, then only eight years old. Later, when Esther had asked Quintin how he'd managed to sit still for so long, he said he'd simply entertained himself with thoughts of a new adventure. She'd pressed him, teasing him that it wasn't very grown up to be woolgathering. He'd only responded by questioning her on the visit; he'd heard and remembered everything that was said.

"Do you not believe so, Lady Esther?"

Oh, drat. Here she was remembering how Quintin could both imagine and pay attention at the same time, to the extent that she was fully distracting herself from the very thing she wished she could do herself. Blast.

"Yes, I believe so," she said. Hopefully that was the right answer.

Lord Copeland nodded solemnly and with unhidden approval. "I knew you would see it my way."

Lord Elles glanced at Esther and shook his head, all faux injury. Esther only smiled and pretended she knew what was happening. Hopefully she hadn't just agreed to something horrible.

A new sound, deep and soft, reached her. The moment she heard it, she knew what it was, though she'd never once heard it before. It stilled her breath and demanded all her attention. Every other voice and sound in the room seemed to fade away until only that one deep rumble remained. Esther glanced over toward the pianoforte to make sure she wasn't wrong.

Quintin was singing.

It wasn't loud, not enough to draw much notice at all, truly. But even clear across the room, Esther couldn't ignore it. Since when did Quintin sing? She couldn't remember ever hearing him do so before. If only there was a valid excuse to cross the room so she could hear him better. Short of *obviously* moving closer only to hear him, she couldn't think of anything. Quintin truly had a fantastic singing voice. Not loud or overbearing, but steady and warm.

His voice called to her; she could lose herself in the sound. Low and steady, his pitch was perfect and the quality was not to be ignored. His gaze came up and met hers. Heat skittered across her chest as his voice seemed to grow stronger. Was he singing to her? Or was that only her hope speaking? The urge to stand and cross the room to him beat against her. At the same time, she felt the unfamiliar sensation of not being able to move at all.

What would it be like to stand and walk up to him? Not just close enough to better hear, but close enough to reach out? Close enough to run her fingers through those sandy waves she so loved?

"Is that Lady Christina at the pianoforte again?" Lord Copeland asked.

Esther blinked. She could not do what she'd imagined; they were in a room full of society, after all. "I believe so," she pushed out.

Lord Copeland tsked, then spoke softly. "I have never known a woman who insists on playing the pianoforte, or any other instrument for so long."

"She only began a few minutes before you gentlemen joined us."

Lord Copeland seemed not to hear her. "I have been sorely tempted more than once to check if her skirt is not glued to the bench."

Esther glanced over at her conversation companion. Such a remark was far harsher than anything she'd heard from Lord Copeland in the past. "Oh no, I will not allow that. She is quite accomplished, you must admit." Even if seeing Quintin making music with her *did* make Esther rather want to stomp her foot and demand someone else take a turn performing.

"Come now, Lady Esther—"

Lady Christina hit a sour note and the song came to a dead halt.

"Oh," Lady Christina laughed, high and tittering. "How very

stupid of me." She tried the passage again and hit the same sour note. "Only this passage," her voice began to shake, "it is quite difficult, I am afraid." It seemed everyone in the room had paused to listen to Lady Christina struggle.

Lord Copeland swirled the brandy inside the cup in his hand. "Mark my word, if you do not get up and insist on having your turn performing, she will be there for the rest of the night, determined to find the right notes."

Lady Christina repeated the same four measures. Though she did not make the same mistake as before, she stumbled in a new way and promptly stopped herself, saying she'd best try again.

"Oh no, Lord Copeland, I do not play," Esther insisted. She'd learned but little as a child. Playing the pianoforte involved far too much sitting still for it ever to be something she could be good at. Painting she could manage, but not the pianoforte.

Lady Christina spoke up, even as her fingers were backtracking to the beginning of those same four measures. "Let me try it one more time. I am sure I will get it right this time—"

"Leave it be, Christina," Lord Copeland called out across the room. "Why, Lady Esther said herself that you've quite consumed the whole of the pianoforte all night. I'm sure she's not the only one who feels so."

"Lord Copeland, please," Esther hissed. How dare he put words in her mouth that way.

Lady Christina looked at him with wide eyes, then looked over at her. Esther wanted to crawl inside the sofa she sat on and never leave. She hadn't said she was tired of hearing Lady Christina play. Not in that way. She most certainly hadn't intended her statement to be announced to all in attendance.

"Lord Copeland." Quintin's voice came out cold and low. "I believe you've had too much brandy, sir." Quintin's gaze moved from Lord Copeland to Esther, and his expression didn't soften.

Esther looked away. After what Lord Copeland said, he must think her a selfish ninny.

Lord Copeland only laughed, though at the sound Esther did

wonder if perhaps he wasn't a tad too far into his cups. "Lud, Tina and I always say what we wish to one another. We're cousins, didn't you know?" He waved off Quintin's objections with a hand. "Besides, I only spoke the truth. No one should take offense at that. Life is what it is."

The statement only made Esther's stomach churn all the more. Her eyes moved back to Quintin. He wasn't watching her. Instead, he had a hand at the small of Lady Christina's back. The poor woman looked close to tears. Slowly, she stood and moved away from the pianoforte, Quintin at her side, whispering; what he whispered exactly, Esther could only guess at.

A myriad of emotions swirled through Esther. Too many to count. Far too many to understand. Quintin stood as close to Lady Christina as he'd stood by her only a few hours before. Possibly even closer. It made Esther's face heat. That was the man she so dearly loved, speaking with and comforting another woman. She shouldn't care. She *couldn't*. Esther had very clearly told Quintin that she wasn't available to him.

Lord Copeland laughed. Esther glanced his way. What had he and Lord Elles been saying? She searched her brain, trying to recall what she'd missed. But there was nothing she could remember.

Esther turned back toward Quintin. Lady Christina was dabbing her eyes with a handkerchief. Was it Quintin's? Esther closed her eyes and forced her head away. She needed to let him go.

But oh, the way Quintin had looked at her. He fully believed Lord Copeland's words, that she had spoken so ill of another woman. He thought less of her for it.

She could explain. No doubt, there would be an opportunity either later tonight or next time they were in company together. But if his good opinion was tainted by him believing she'd *spoken* ill of Lady Christina, there was no chance it would survive him learning what she'd *done* in India. The breath in her throat thickened until she couldn't swallow. Her lungs burned as she fought against her need to heave for air. This was exactly what she wanted to avoid. She could tolerate nearly anything, but she could not stand for

Quintin to learn that she wasn't as brave as the heroes they'd pretended to be as children.

He, on the other hand, was every bit as kind and magnanimous as they'd proclaimed themselves to be all those years ago. No doubt, he was brave and brilliant too.

But not her. Esther was a coward. She'd buckled and no doubt would again, someday. A woman like her was too addle-brained to be a hero. She'd wanted to be more—oh gads, but she'd wanted to grow up into a gracious, generous woman. She'd wanted to be like the heroes in the stories Quintin had told her.

But she'd failed. And there was no going back.

One could not fix the past, as one could mend a tear in a dress or re-pin a lock of fallen hair. When one *acted,* it was permanent.

Esther blinked a few times and forced herself to be aware of the others in the room. She could not dissolve into tears here. Lady Christina was beside two other women, speaking softly. They seemed quite sympathetic toward her, and one even threw a glare Esther's direction. Quintin was no longer beside her, but the realization didn't do anything to soothe Esther's own ill-thinking toward herself. She glanced about and found him standing beside Lord Dunn, speaking with the elderly man. He didn't look her way. He seemed to have fully forgotten about her.

Why should he not?

Esther reached out and placed a hand on her mother's arm. "Excuse me, Mother, but I have a terrible headache coming on," Esther lied. "I feel it would be best I return home."

Mother eyed her closely. "You didn't eat too much at supper, did you?"

Lords Copeland and Elles were listening in as well. Esther did her best to ignore them. "No, of course not. I think it is only all the comings and goings of a London Season. I am quite worn out."

"Another headache, Lady Esther?" Lord Copeland said, leaning toward her. "I hope it does not turn out to be anything too serious."

"No." She shook her head. "I'm only in need of a good night's sleep and I am sure I shall be well once more." It was a delicate balance between not raising alarm yet still convincing Mother to allow her to return home.

Mother's lips pulled first one direction and then the other. "Very well," she said with a sigh. Esther felt bad pulling Mother away when she so loved company, but she couldn't stay here any longer. Mother said her farewells to several people as they made their way ever so slowly toward the door.

After listening to Mother tell several ladies of indeterminant age about the room to please come visit during their at-home tomorrow, Esther's head began to truly pound. She felt it just punishment for her lie. When she returned home, she wouldn't even try to make it go away. She deserved no less.

Mother finally took hold of Esther's arm and they began what she hoped was finally their exit from the room. Quintin hadn't glanced at her once the entire time. As they neared the door, their path brought them quite close to Lady Christina. The two women beside Lady Christina turned their noses up at Esther as her mother's path brought them closer together.

Esther kept her eye on the door. The sooner she left this whole evening behind her the better. First Quintin's nearness had upended her, then his attentions to Lady Christina had hurt her, immediately followed by Lord Copeland's words which had shocked and embarrassed her.

It was certainly time to go home.

Still, something in her stomach bade her stop. Pausing just inside the door, Esther took a deep breath. Releasing Mother's arm —and praying mother wouldn't take this opportunity to delve into a fifteen-minute-long conversation with one of her many friends— Esther retraced her steps. No one in the room seemed to be paying her any mind, which was the only blessing Esther could reasonably hope for.

She stopped in front of Lady Christina, not daring to look either of the other women in the eyes. "Pardon me, Lady Christina."

Lady Christina didn't answer, but her lips pursed tight and Esther got the distinct impression she wasn't wanted.

"Please know," Esther began, keeping her voice low, "That I said no such thing to your cousin. In fact, I told Lord Quintin only a few weeks ago that you are quite the most accomplished player I have ever heard."

Lady Christina didn't respond, but she didn't seem so hurt either.

There seemed nothing else to say, so Esther curtsied and hurried to catch up to Mother. From somewhere in the room, she felt certain Quintin was watching her. The feeling brought tears to her eyes, though she couldn't rightly say why. Taking her mother's arm once more, she hurried them both out of the room. She couldn't get home fast enough.

CHAPTER 14

*E*sther slowly turned before the long mirror in her room. Her ballgown flowed and rustled and glistened about her.

"Oh, my lady," Joan said in a sing-song voice. "I'm sure you've been dreaming of this night for years and years."

"I have," Esther responded truthfully. What girl didn't dream of her coming-out ball? Only, now that it was here, it didn't feel at all like she'd imagined. She'd always thought she'd be swept up in the magic of the moment, the thrill of knowing her whole life was in front of her, the pulsing excitement at wondering who had come, who would dance with her, whose eyes she'd catch.

In the end, she'd always seen herself descending the stairs and finding Quintin standing there, tall and handsome, dressed impeccably. He'd ask her to dance. She would say yes.

The rest had always disappeared into a blur of her and him and the stars in the night sky.

"I think you need a different necklace."

Esther glanced over to find Joan looking her up and down quite critically.

"You want to look your best and all that," the abigail said, moving out of the room.

Esther turned back to the mirror and looked harder. She didn't feel very pretty tonight. The dress was right, and her hair was quite fashionably done up. But ever since the Monstattens' supper party, she'd felt ugly. She ought to have felt ugly all along, after how she had told Lieutenant Fallow about Lady Helen. Lord Copeland may have twisted her words the other night—a fact he had apologized for more than once since—but even having a room full of people *think* that's what she'd said had made her feel awful. What would they all think if they knew what she'd done in India? Esther shook her head. She wasn't a lady at all. She was a mean hypocrite.

"Here we are." Joan entered the room again, a long strand of pearls in her hands. "These will be perfect. The white will offset your dark hair and draw attention to your eyes."

"You are very kind, Joan," was all Esther could manage to say.

"Nonsense. Only doing my job. Now," she stepped back, "what do you think?"

The pearls did look wonderful. "They're perfect."

Joan moved up close to Esther and sighed. "What I wouldn't give to go down there with you tonight, my lady. To see all the men stop and stare. I bet you won't sit out a single dance."

"I hope not. It is my own coming-out ball, after all."

Joan only sighed again. The young woman was rather partial to that wordless sentiment.

"Do you have your eye on one man in particular, my lady?"

Esther stopped her brain before it threw up images of Quintin, particularly those of him dancing with her in his arms. Or those of him singing, with her this time, at the pianoforte. "No."

"Not even one Lord Copeland?" Joan waggled her eyebrows.

"Oh Joan, please."

Joan only laughed. "I think I guessed at your secret."

Hardly. "We are good friends. But I believe that is all."

"For now. You two did spend quite a long time in the gardens the other day."

"He was apologizing."

"Oh? What for? Trying to kiss you?"

"Joan!" Where did the young woman come up with these things? Esther's earlier worry that everyone was talking of her and Lord Copeland as a couple came back in full force. It was followed closely by an even worse thought—suppose Lord Copeland *did* try to kiss her? Esther shuddered and forced the idea away. "Of course not. A few nights previous, he'd made an unkind comment and he only wanted to let me know how sorry he was."

Joan nodded as though she was all knowing; where was the shy, uncertain woman from when they had discussed Will? Esther was sorely tempted to bring him up in the hopes it would still Joan's tongue a bit. But she didn't want Joan to feel she couldn't speak her mind, and she most assuredly didn't want to risk her words hurting another woman. So Esther kept Will out of it.

"It must have been quite the apology," Joan crooned.

Lord Copeland had been sincerely apologetic. Though he hadn't said so directly, Esther easily surmised his evening had not gone any better than hers. Apparently, he hadn't been happy to arrive at the Monstattens' only to find Quintin and Esther speaking so closely. During supper, he'd not missed her frequent glances Quintin's way—much to Esther's mortification. Then, after returning to the parlor, he'd found a distant and distracted Esther. He'd only been upset, and quite possibly a little drunk, and acted in a way he sorely regretted later.

He'd promised her he'd already made his most sincere apologies to Lady Christina and only hoped she'd forgive him as well. She'd readily agreed, though her own guilt had not been so easily assuaged.

"Come," Joan said, moving to the bedchamber door. "I believe they are ready for you."

They probably were. But that didn't mean Esther was ready for *them*. Still, she moved toward the door. Lord Copeland would be here tonight, of that she had no doubt. Would Quintin? They hadn't seen one another since the Monstattens' supper party. Did he remember that tonight they had hoped to get Joan and Will some time to speak with one another? She wouldn't blame him if he cried off and refused to help her in such an inane scheme now.

Esther reached the top of the stairs and looked down at the gathered party below. There, standing just where she'd always dreamed he'd be, was Quintin. At the sight of him, all the nervousness faded. She took the first step just as he looked up. Their eyes met and held. She could see several unpleasant emotions rolling about inside of him. They needed to speak about the supper party. She needed him to know what she *had* said, not what Lord Copeland had announced she'd said.

It seemed though, that the closer to the base of the stairs she moved, the more individuals crowded in between her and Quintin. She was not nearly as tall as the men about the space, she wasn't even as tall as most of the other women. As Esther stepped down off the bottom stair, she lost sight of Quintin. First one woman, then a man, then another man, and then another woman, all greeted her and stole a few minutes of her time to congratulate her; on her coming out, on her beauty, on several other pointless things all of which Esther struggled to focus on.

The crowd about her parted briefly and she caught sight of Quintin. He'd not moved from his spot near the ballroom door. Why wouldn't he come to her? Esther tried to move his direction, but then another elderly woman took her elbow and began speaking. Esther responded kindly, repeatedly glancing over at Quintin. He stood alone, and he clearly saw her. His eyes seemed to never leave her. Yet, he didn't move.

Why should he though? She'd given him no indication that she wanted him by her side. Esther's stomach turned sour and she couldn't help but worry whether she truly could make it through tonight. Then Mother was suddenly by her side.

"Esther, child, gracious. Why didn't you send someone for me the moment you were ready to come down?" Quickly and determinedly, Mother steered Esther around Quintin and into the ballroom through another door. Esther wasn't sure if Mother had done so for the express purpose of keeping her away from Quintin, or simply because this door was more likely to draw attention. Either way, she didn't see him again for several dances.

Had he quitted the ball entirely? Was he standing up with other women? Lady Christina, perhaps? Lady Christina was prone to talking on and on without breath, granted, but she was a good woman, nonetheless. Esther could find no fault in her character. Quintin deserved a good woman like that.

The midnight waltz came and went. Esther stood up with Lord Copeland, much to her mother's pleasure. Lord Copeland, for his part, was quite on his best behavior. He spoke only compliments regarding those around him and not an ill word slipped his tongue. Though he never said anything truly interesting, he was all politeness, and Esther was glad for it. Even if she was a little bored.

The hours moved by. Joan's prediction turned out to be prophetic; Esther sat out for not a single dance. Still, she didn't see Quintin, not once, since she'd first descended the stairs. As three in the morning neared, the ballroom began to thin, though it was still stiflingly hot.

"Do you think the rest of our guests will retire soon?" Esther asked her mother as they sat along the dance floor between sets. She both wanted everyone to leave and didn't at the same time. She did enjoy dancing, and she was finding some pleasure in all the attention. But she was also disappointed to not have stood up at all with Quintin, nor have the opportunity to explain.

Mother shook her head. "Not for another hour or two is my guess."

Another matron sitting beside Mother spoke up. "Everyone is having such a grand time, I wouldn't be surprised if we're still here when the sun rises."

"Yes," a third matron, to Esther's left, said. "Very well done, Lady Harrington. Very well done indeed."

Esther sat up a bit straighter. She couldn't expect Lord Dunn to stay that long. He was quite elderly, after all. She hadn't been sure about trying to get Joan and Will some time together without Quintin's help. But the more she'd wrestled with the idea the more confident she felt. She could do this. If she didn't, there might not be another chance. When else was she certain to have Lord Dunn here with his driver?

"Pardon me." Esther broke into the conversation that her mother and the other two matrons had started up in her silence. "But I fear the flowers in my hair are wilting in the heat of the room."

Mother took hold of her chin and turned her head around, inspecting the flowers which Joan had carefully placed. "They don't look too wilted to me."

"Look closer, Lady Harrington," one of the matrons said. "Here, and this one"—Esther could feel the lady poking her hair—"and that one isn't too fresh looking either."

"I don't see what we can do about it now," Mother said, letting go of her head, allowing Esther to face forward once more.

"I'll go get Joan. She and I can pick a few new flowers in no time at all." Esther stood. "You do want me to look my finest tonight, right? Since this is my coming-out ball and all."

"Well, of course, my dear," Mother said, her tone proving she wasn't fully convinced. "But you cannot be gone as long as all that."

Esther addressed all three of the matrons. "Would you please explain to anyone who asks? Perhaps even to those who don't ask, to keep the gossipmongers at bay?"

The elderly matron who'd been sitting to Esther's left laughed, a dry wheezing sort of sound, but not an unpleasant one.

"Yes, little one," the other matron sitting beside Mother said. "You go freshen up your flowers; we'll keep the gossip at bay. Your absence will only make the gentlemen long for your return. Don't you agree, Lady Harrington?"

Mother, lips pulled to the side, watched Esther closely for a silent minute. Did Mother suspect she was up to *more* than simply replacing the flowers in her hair? Mother had never been particularly untrusting. Normally she allowed Esther most anything she wished, but there were moments when her looks made Esther

wonder if she couldn't somehow peer into the deepest, most
hidden parts of her imagination and peruse all of Esther's wild
wishes unchecked.

"Very well," she finally said, sitting back in her chair. "Only
don't be gone too long and be sure Joan is with you for the entire
time."

"Thank you, Mother." Esther gave all three women a quick
curtsy and then hurried through the ballroom and up the stairs,
back into her room. She may not be able to give Joan and Will long
—her mother was right in that if she stayed away for long there
would be nothing which kept the gossipmongers silent—but she
could give them something.

"Joan?" she called out the minute she reached her room.

The abigail slipped back into Esther's room at the second call.
"Done for the night already, my lady?" Joan asked, surprised.

"No, actually. I need your help. My flowers are a bit wilted."
Esther didn't wait for Joan to assess the blooms for herself, and
instead reached back and began plucking them out of her hair.

"Hold up, my lady." Joan hurried around and behind Esther.
"Don't go pulling out your locks with the blooms." Joan began
pulling them out one by one.

"After you've removed them all, we'll go down near the stables
and pick a few new ones."

"Are you sure?" Joan asked. "Won't that take time away from
your dancing?"

Esther shrugged. "I'd rather look my best than get in yet one
more dance."

"If you wish it, my lady."

It was providential that tonight was her own coming-out ball; it
meant no one thought twice about her insisting even the flowers in
her hair looked fresh and perfect. Soon, the discarded flowers were
piled atop her vanity table and the two of them hurried through the
house, purposely avoiding most of the guests, and stepped outside.
The night was warm, one of the first truly warm nights of spring. It

was exciting, but also hinted at an oppressive summer to come. Would she still be in London come July or even August when the heat pinched and the air seemed to stick to one's skin? Some ladies, who were not successful in obtaining an offer before, did stick around, preferring that to requiring an entire Season again the following year. Esther took hold of Joan's arm and hurried them forward.

She didn't want to think about her own offers or opportunities just now. The only thing she wanted to focus on was Joan and Joan's offers and opportunities. With any luck, tonight would prove quite profitable in that area.

"I noticed some lovely Rockcress blooms near the stables this morning," she said.

Joan only nodded. It didn't take long to find the flowers. The plant came up not even past Esther's knees, and were all topped with the most delicate, white flowers. Candlelight spilled from inside the stable, making the night less impossible to see in, though the flowers remained mostly in shadow. Esther bent over and began plucking a few blooms.

"We'll want to gather extra," Joan said. "Just to be safe."

"Good idea." They worked side by side for only a few minutes before Joan stood up once more.

"That should do. Let us return and see if we can't have you ready before the next set begins."

Not yet. Esther remained bent over, inspecting a flower. They couldn't go back in before Joan had the opportunity to speak with Will. Otherwise, this whole adventure would be for naught. Joan was out here with her, and Will was most likely just inside the stable. But how to get Joan *inside*?

Esther stood and held out her small handful of flowers. "I can't tell if any of these looks right or not. It's just too dark."

"I'm sure most of them will be just fine. If some aren't, that's why we picked extra."

She couldn't let Joan return to the house just yet. "Would you please take these inside the stable? There's plenty of light in there and you can look over the petals and make sure they are what we need."

It was hard to see much in the night, even with a little light coming from the stable, but Joan appeared to be thinking it over.

"Please, Joan," Esther pressed. "I don't want to return to the house only to have to send you back out here again. It'll only take a minute."

Joan dropped a brief curtsy. "Very well, my lady. If you wish it." Esther poured her flowers into Joan's cupped hands and the abigail moved around the building, heading for the stable doors. Esther bit softly against her bottom lip. This was it. Wait—suppose Will *wasn't* inside? She had no idea where else he'd be, but there was a chance she was wrong about him being in the stable.

Esther followed Joan's path. She reached the large, open stable doors and peered inside. Joan stood near Esther's mount, Lily Bay, her head bent over her open hands. There was a bit of noise from deeper in the stable. Will strode into view. Esther knew the moment he caught sight of Joan; his form stilled and then he smiled softly.

Walk over and talk to her, walk over and talk to her, Esther silently pleaded with him.

She couldn't tell if Joan knew of his presence or not. Most likely she didn't, since Joan hadn't looked up from the flowers in her hands even once. If Will let this hand-molded opportunity pass him by then Esther didn't know what she would do. Perhaps the man was too much of a coward to speak up? Just because he was willing to save Joan when she was stuck in the loft, didn't mean he was willing to continue the connection. Esther placed a hand against the outside stable doorframe. Please, one of them needed to do something. She had gotten them together, but she couldn't force them to *speak*. Her fingers began rapping against her leg. She stilled them instantly. The last thing she needed was to get caught here—that would most certainly end any chance Joan and Will had of conversing tonight.

Joan stood up straight and, turning slightly, looked as though she was heading back out the stable door. Esther felt herself tense.

This was it. She had no more stories left, nothing else to use to keep Joan and Will close to each other. Will hurried forward suddenly, his boots striking the dirt floor with a low thump-thump.

Joan turned at the noise, away from Esther so she could no longer see her abigail's face.

"Good evening," Will said, pulling the hat off his head.

Joan replied, but too softly for Esther to hear. Esther sighed in relief. They were finally speaking.

"He waited until the last second, didn't he?"

The deep, masculine voice made Esther jump.

She spun around. Quintin stood just to the side, also peering into the stable. "How long have you been here?"

"I saw you and Joan slip out of the house. You know it's bad form to go adventuring without your partner in crime."

Joan and Will seemed to have slipped into an easy sort of conversation, so Esther pulled away from the door so she might speak more openly with Quintin. "I thought after the Monstattens' supper party that you wouldn't want to speak with me."

He followed her lead, moving around the corner of the stable and closer once more to the white Rockcress flowers. "I was under the impression that it was *you* who did not wish to speak to *me*." He said it in a straightforward manner, but Esther didn't miss the tightness about the words nor the way the sentence ended a touch abruptly.

She'd hurt him. Again.

"Please let me explain," she said. "Lord Copeland twisted my words. I hadn't said I was tired of hearing Lady Christina playing. I'd only commented that she'd begun before the men joined us. Lord Copeland made up the rest."

Quintin listened in silence. Esther waited for a minute for him to say something, but he didn't.

"He did apologize to me the following morning," Esther added. She didn't like silence. "He told me he had already apologized to Lady Christina as well. I don't think he meant any harm by it." Why wasn't Quintin saying anything? Normally, Quintin wasn't as quiet with her as he was with others. Not only that, but the few times he did need his silence, it had never bothered Esther.

At least, that's the way it used to be.

She suddenly didn't feel like *that* Esther and he wasn't *that* Quintin anymore. He was withdrawing, even from her.

But Quintin probably saw the whole situation in quite a different light.

She was allowing another man to openly court her. Quintin had a deep, melodious voice she'd never heard before the other night, and she'd taken on tonight's adventure without even trying to include him.

"I'm sorry, Quintin." She wasn't fully sure why she was apologizing, but she felt she needed to. Perhaps for her small part in Lord Copeland's inexcusable behavior of the other night. Perhaps simply for growing up and not becoming the woman she'd always promised herself she'd be.

"Esther, what are we doing?" Quintin finally asked.

She almost said that they were giving Joan and Will a chance to speak with one another, but she stopped herself. That wasn't what he meant, and she knew it.

He moved closer to her, taking her hand in his. "You remember the willow tree and my promise to you?"

It was just like when she'd first arrived at the Monstattens'. The air between them suddenly came alive, whispering rousing tales of how close Quintin was to her, and how wondrous it would be if she leaned in just a little more.

He cupped a hand around her cheek. "What changed?"

Esther blinked several times. Her heart raced so loudly she could barely think. Did she dare tell him? How would he respond? Memories of his stern scowl pressed out any hope that he would understand. She had knowingly hurt another woman. Acted the coward and thrown another in the way so that she might escape. Quintin, who was ever the gentleman and the hero, ever standing up for others and putting their needs before his own—there was a very good chance he would never understand or forgive her.

"You know," Quintin whispered, "I'd intended to kiss you properly the day we met under the willow tree. Only, I chickened out at the last minute." Slowly his thumb began to rub softly against her cheek—the very spot he'd kissed so many years ago. "Would you mind terribly if I didn't chicken out this time?" He leaned down, bringing them ever so much closer.

His lips met hers.

Oh, heaven. It was even more wonderful than she'd imagined. The kiss was soft, light. Yet it sent her heart pounding. Every inch of her ached to lean in closer, to kiss him back with all the fervor she felt rushing through her. To run her fingers through his hair and—

Lady Helen Fallow's face came to mind, her wedding veil unsuccessfully hiding her sorrow. Even as Quintin's arms wrapped around her and he pulled her against him, Esther's stomach turned sour.

She placed a hand on his chest and pulled back. "Quintin, don't."

He stopped instantly, freezing beside her. The warmth she'd felt from him moments ago transformed into painful uncertainty.

"Please, I can't." She couldn't do this any longer. She couldn't string him along, allowing him to believe they could ever be together. He would never understand. He would never forgive. But at least she could cut him free and allow him to find happiness elsewhere.

His arm dropped back to his side and he rocked back.

Esther reached out and took hold of his hand. "I'm so sorry. It's just that—" She squeezed her eyes shut; how did one even go about this? "I met a lieutenant in India. He ... I . . ." The words choked her throat. She had to get them out, had to end both of their misery. "I thought I could hide the past." If only she could make him understand. But the shame and intense need to keep her secret swirled about her, clouding her thoughts. "That was India, this is England. I thought I could come back and pretend none of it ever happened." Drat. She wasn't making any sense; she was certain she wasn't.

"You forgot me," he said, his words hollow, and they seemed to echo about her own chest, knocking against her ribs and bruising her heart. "Just like everyone else."

No. No. It wasn't at all like that.

"My lady?"

Esther whirled around at Joan's voice. Quintin pulled his hand free of hers in the process. The moment the contact was lost, Esther missed it. Her hand was cold without him holding it. *She* was cold.

Joan stood only a few paces off, Will beside her. "Are you quite all right?" she asked.

"Yes, Joan." Did she look as upset as she felt? "Lord Quintin and I were only having a friendly conversation."

"Do you still wish me to fix the flowers in your hair?" Poor Joan. She seemed quite confused as to what she was expected to do. This probably wasn't a situation many abigails found themselves in.

Esther glanced back over at Quintin. He was looking at her, but in the dark, she couldn't see his eyes. What she wouldn't give to be able to know exactly what he was thinking just now.

"If you will excuse me, Lady Esther," he said at length, "I'll just see to my own horse and then I shall leave you be."

Not giving her time to respond, he strode by her, Joan, and Will and disappeared into the stable. Esther remained rooted to the spot.

Joan walked forward, resting her hand against Esther's arm. "Come, my lady, let's get you inside and back to your ball."

Oh gracious, there was still a ball going on in her honor. She couldn't return looking as though she'd been doing anything untoward. Were her eyes as puffy as they felt? Esther nodded, and allowed Joan to pull her back toward the house. With every step she took, Quintin's words echoed about her mind.

You forgot me. Just like everyone else.

CHAPTER 15

*Q*uintin lay with his hands behind his head, elbows stretched out, the bed quilt kicked down next to his bare feet. Sunlight crested the windowsill and slipped its brilliant rays across his bedchamber floor. He'd hardly slept at all since quitting the ball last night.

Esther had met someone.

A lieutenant, apparently. Did he treat her well? Perhaps flatter her with compliments and shower her with flowers? Quintin himself had never been a lavish sycophant. He'd never really wondered if praise and accolades were important to Esther. It seemed now that he should have. Did this lieutenant make her feel safe? Did he hold her close and help her see that it was her gumption and spunk that made her so beautiful? Surely she wouldn't willingly attach herself to a man who thought she should be forever subdued and demure, much like her own mother wished her to be. Surely not. Right?

Or perhaps she'd simply decided that their adventures were beneath her. That his inexplicable love for stories and heroes was childish. Perhaps she'd only not said so outright in an effort to be kind. She'd warned him weeks ago that she was not who she'd been, had she not? She'd tried most generously to put him on his guard. He should have heeded her warnings.

Instead, he'd continued on, hoping like a fool's fool, that she would change back to the Esther he'd known. Hoping that she would remember why they'd been such good friends, and how perfectly they fit into one another's lives. Not only that, but last night he'd learned through experience what he'd always assumed, that he and Esther also fit perfectly well in each other's arms.

The room was growing lighter by the minute. Quintin had not moved in what must have been close to an hour. It was as though every muscle in his legs, torso, and arms were weighed down. He was being pressed tightly against the bed, his own turmoil not allowing him to toss or turn or move on.

And that was it. He couldn't move on. He was stuck in the past, hoping and willing Esther to return to their childhood with him. Wanting beyond anything else for her to stay with him, just as she always had when they were young.

But she had moved on. She'd left and forgotten him long ago.

Everyone always forgot Quintin eventually. He'd just always thought she was the exception to that rule.

Quintin let out a heavy breath. He couldn't force her to be with him, and he didn't want to. If she was needing to let him go, then he wouldn't hold her back. He had no desire to turn into a cage for Esther or anyone.

Should he write her and let her know he was returning to Cottonhold? He'd overheard Lady Harrington tell more than one of her friends that she would be at-home today, despite staying up late for the ball, and they ought to drop by. Quintin's lips ticked up in a bitter grin; he should have known better than allowing his quiet heart to fall for the daughter of a society-hungry butterfly.

No. He wouldn't write or call. Either could send the wrong message throughout society that he had designs on Esther. Doing either would likely also make Esther uncomfortable.

Quintin was going to let Esther go—and he wouldn't do it in a way that made her other options harder to obtain.

He would leave this very morning. She'd find out of his departing London soon enough and she'd understand that he was wishing her well.

With a firm course of action in mind, Quintin rolled to the side and sat up. His feet brushed against the soft rug which extended out from under his bed. Cottonhold was where he belonged. It was time he returned.

Standing, he rung for his valet. The sooner he took his leave of London, the better. Venetia would, no doubt, accuse him of hiding. Well, she could think what she willed. He'd see to it that she had a comfortable coach to ride in, whether she chose to accompany him to Cottonhold or return to Ramport Manor. Either way, he wanted to ride horseback. He needed some wide, open sky and uncrowded road to clear his head.

LESS THAN AN HOUR LATER, QUINTIN WAS DOWN IN THE STABLES readying his horse. Venetia had not even arisen yet, but he was determined to have everything ready to go so the moment she *was* up, they could be on their way. John would be happy Quintin had decided to return to Cottonhold.

An image of John, sitting across Quintin at the supper table, with a less-grim-than-usual expression on his face came forcibly to Quintin.

That's what he had to look forward to.

Quintin leaned against his horse and shook his head. Esther had made her decision. He wasn't going to force her into anything. If she'd wanted him, she'd had plenty of times to tell him so. A soft crack echoed from the direction of the house. Quintin held still and listened.

There it was again.

He couldn't identify the sound; it sounded nothing like anything he'd heard before. Glancing over his horse, Quintin found all to be in order and the stall secure. He left the stables and walked out into the morning light.

A horse stood, grazing peacefully, tied to a tree. The mare looked markedly like Esther's horse, Lily Bay. Quintin hurried his pace.

A solitary figure stood facing the south hall of the house. She leaned back, arm held away from her, and then flung her closed hand forward. A soft plink echoed over the lawn.

Quintin shook his head and demanded that the surge of hope that skittered through him be still. Esther had come to throw pebbles at his bedchamber window. That was a far cry from her announcing she'd been in the wrong and wanted to be with him now.

He moved quietly toward her, even as Esther bent down and searched the grass for another pebble. Rearing back, she tossed that one after the others. Only, it missed and hit the wall beside the window instead.

"Drat," she whispered softly.

Did she still use that word? She had as a child, until one day her mother had heard her using it. Quintin had never had his own mouth cleaned out with soap, but it hadn't appeared to be a pleasant experience.

"Me thinks," he said out loud, even as she jumped at the sound of his voice, "that your Juliet sleeps quite heavily."

Esther whirled around and faced him. She looked lovely. Granted, her eyes were a bit puffy and her face seemed more pale than usual. But she was still lovely. She was always lovely.

"*Don't* sneak up on me like that." She pressed both fists down.

"My apologies." Then again, if she'd been less prone to forget him, perhaps she wouldn't be so surprised when he suddenly showed up.

She took in a trembling breath, her fingers finding each other and twisting about. "I thought you would still be abed."

"I couldn't sleep."

Why was she here? She'd made her wishes perfectly clear the night before.

"Neither could I," she said. Her fingers moved on from twisting about each other to messing with the edge of her jacket. "I felt we should talk. Without servants or anyone else around."

He couldn't disagree more. Quintin felt no desire to hear her describe, in painful detail, why her affections had switched from him to another. "Then let me start. I'm leaving today."

"Leaving?"

Why she bothered to look upset he didn't care to imagine. "I'm returning to Cottonhold where I belong."

"You are?"

He was pretty sure he'd just said he was. He wouldn't have said it if he hadn't meant it.

Esther's hands moved through a variety of actions. They twisted together, they fingered her skirt, they even disappeared behind her back for a moment, though he knew they were far from still even then.

"When will you be returning?" she finally asked.

Returning? He shook his head. He had no plans to ever return to London.

She took a step forward, bringing her quite close. "Surely you mean to return."

He could smell the soft scent of flowers on her, just like last night. They were grown now, yet she still barely came to his shoulder. She was all he'd ever wanted. He'd never even bothered looking at another.

Yet, Esther had.

Quintin shook his head again. He needed to leave, and he wasn't going to allow himself to even think of returning. Tears lined the bottom of her eyes. Quintin's arms ached to reach out and pull her close. He didn't understand why she was crying; hadn't she told him herself that she'd met someone else? Nonetheless, he hated the thought of her so upset.

He reached out and placed a hand against her arm. She didn't pull away, but neither did she lean in. Her words from last night hit against him once more.

His hand dropped away. "I am sure you and your lieutenant will—"

"*My* lieutenant?" Esther's sudden, shocked outburst stilled Quintin's next words. Her eyes were wide, even while her brows and lips twisted into something he could only identify as revulsion.

"Yes?" he asked slowly. Wasn't that what she had told him last night?

"Oh, he isn't *my* lieutenant." She seemed to shudder at the thought.

Hold on. Quintin watched her closely, the whole world seeming to shift beneath him. She *wasn't* holding a tendre for this mystery soldier. No, there was something completely different at play here.

"Did you think . . .?" Esther half-asked, then covered her face with one hand. She turned away. Turned back. "I knew I wasn't making much sense last night."

Quintin felt he ought to be elated, but he wasn't. No matter who this lieutenant was or what had happened in India, Esther had still kept him at arm's length ever since her return. She wasn't jumping into his arms now, either. The only thing he knew for certain was that he knew nothing about what had been truly bothering Esther ever since she had returned home.

"What happened in India?" he asked, though his words sounded more like pleading.

For the first time that morning—perhaps ever—Esther grew still. Her arms folded tightly against her and she looked up from beneath her lashes. She looked horribly sad. The look on her face mixed in Quintin's mind with the way she'd shuddered when he'd called the mystery soldier "your lieutenant".

Something hard heaved inside Quintin. "Did he hurt you?"

"No." Her voice was so very soft, Quintin could barely hear. "But he wanted to."

Quintin didn't stop himself this time. He wrapped his arms completely around her, holding her close to his chest. Did Lord and Lady Harrington know? Had they not done *anything* to protect their only daughter? Anger and the heady need to protect Esther flooded through him. It was a deuced good thing for the lieutenant that he wasn't present.

"He *didn't* hurt you though?" Quintin needed reassurance.

She shook her head against his chest.

Quintin let out a slow breath. She was all right. She wasn't hurt after all. He rubbed a hand in small circles across her back. He wished she'd told him sooner. Then again, they'd not once had a moment truly alone before now. He wouldn't have been allowed to hold her thus if others had been about.

Esther started to cry. She shook against him with silent sobs.

Quintin pressed a kiss to the top of her head. "It's over now." He hoped the words were soothing. He'd never believed himself to be very good at reassurances. "He won't try to hurt you again."

Esther shook her head again, harder this time. "I did something, Quintin. Something horrible."

"To the lieutenant?" If the man ever crossed Quintin's path, Quintin would most certainly "do something" as well.

"Yes, but no."

All the confusion of the season flared up again, like a raging fire one thought had been put out. "How about you tell me everything?"

"You'll hate me."

He sincerely doubted it. "Just tell me."

Words poured out of her, slowly at first, but quickly picking up speed. She talked of loving India and how she had left England ready to prove herself a grand adventuress. She had been confident she would prove a great boon to her ailing Uncle and see a whole new part of the world at the same time. She even admitted to looking forward to returning and making him green with envy for all the excitement she'd experienced without him. But then she'd been introduced to one Lieutenant Fallow.

Quintin tensed the moment he heard the man's name.

Lieutenant Fallow had soon shown a preference for her. She'd tried to be polite, to kindly dissuade him. She'd even gone to her mother once, asking for help in avoiding him all together. But her request was ignored; Quintin reminded himself he was to always be a gentleman and not think *too many* ill things about Lady Harrington. A half dozen would have to suffice.

Esther spoke on about a midnight picnic. Quintin had heard such things were commonplace enough in India, where it never truly cooled. She spoke of unexpectedly finding herself alone with Lieutenant Fallow. Though she didn't say she'd been scared or frightened or panicked, Quintin could hear it in her tone. The blackguard had put her in a most vulnerable position, all for his own gain. Perhaps Quintin *would* go see India and stop by the lieutenant's post while he was at it.

"I didn't know what to do," Esther said. "He wouldn't let me go. There were others about the gardens; it was only a minute before we would be discovered. I was trapped." She stopped, her head resting fully against his chest.

Quintin didn't interrupt or press her to continue. Instead, he just held her. She would speak when she was ready.

"I did the only thing I could think of to do." Her voice was even softer than before. "I told him it would be easier for him to force Lady Helen into a marriage."

"Lady Helen?" Esther hadn't mentioned the woman before.

"Her father is my Uncle's superior. I think she'd arrived in India just before me. We'd spoken several times, but we never got to know each other very well. She was always so quiet."

So was Quintin. But there was something more. Something else Esther was yet still hesitant to admit. "What did Fallow do?"

"Exactly like I hoped." She didn't sound pleased, but devastated. "He left me be. He walked away and left me alone. A few minutes later I returned to Mother and no one ever knew he'd cornered me."

Relief beat a soft rhythm in Quintin's chest. It wasn't enough to beat out his anger at Fallow, but it was still present. "I am glad."

"But I did it on purpose."

"What?"

"I pushed him toward Lady Helen."

Why was she upset about Fallow leaving her be? "You were protecting yourself. You were clever and thought out a solution." After so many years playing at battling monsters, he wasn't surprised she'd strategized a way to safety.

"No." She pulled back slightly, looking him in the eyes for the first time since she'd begun her tale. "Lady Helen was quiet and submissive. I knew she'd be easy prey. I *knew* it, Quintin. I had a fighting chance at least, but not her. And I pushed him toward her."

"To save *yourself.*"

"That doesn't make it right." Her arms were tight against her chest again as she stepped backward, breaking away from him. She pressed her eyes shut, sending two tears running down her cheeks. "It wasn't right."

"What happened to Lady Helen?"

"She was forced to marry Lieutenant Fallow not long after."

So that, then, was the main cause of her guilt. "To avoid marrying him yourself, you made sure he married another."

She nodded. "Against her will."

No wonder she had been so unpredictable since returning home. For one with as kind and sympathetic a heart as Esther, such knowledge had to be eating her from the inside out.

"You know the worst of it?" she continued, dropping her gaze to the half-frozen grass between them. "Since that night, I've thought of at least five other ways I could have avoided marrying the lieutenant myself while still sparing Lady Helen. I could have pretended I'd seen a snake, screamed, and ran. I could have tried harder to rejoin Mother. I could—"

"Esther, stop."

"But I *could have.* I could have thought of a better out. I *should* have."

"You did the only thing you could think of at the time. Now you need to let it lie."

She shook her head furiously, her dark brown curls bouncing about. "I can't. I can't walk away and forget."

Quintin stepped forward, intent on holding her once more. She needed to understand that what she'd done was sad, yes, but not unforgiveable.

Before he could reach her, Esther moved away further. "And that's why you and I ... Why we can't ever . . ."

Quintin tilted his head to the side. What did Fallow and Lady Helen have to do with him and Esther being together?

"I don't deserve to be with someone I love," she whispered.

No. He couldn't allow that. Such an idea was ridiculous.

She still didn't look up at him. "I feel so much more guilt when I'm around you. Knowing what it's like to be with someone who cares only reminds me what I took from Lady Helen."

"So, you're what? Going to marry someone like Fallow?" Or Lord Copeland, perhaps?

"I have to marry. But that doesn't change the fact that I don't deserve love."

"That's absurd. Esther, you can't—"

"It's good you're leaving, Quintin." She looked up at him finally. Her mouth was set, her eyes red but steady. "You need to go find someone as kind and generous as you. Someone who isn't a coward."

"I don't *want* anyone else."

"All the daydreaming in the world won't make me the woman you want me to be."

Is that what she thought? That he imagined her to be something she wasn't? That his love of story had grown to cloud his vision of her? "All I want is you beside me."

She took another step back. "I can't, Quintin. I'm sorry. Life isn't a fairytale and I'm not your princess." Turning fully around, Esther ran.

CHAPTER 16

Quintin's valet held up two different jackets, one a dark forest green, the other charcoal. Quintin rocked his head back and forth. Neither seemed right for today. Though it was probably just his own unrest manifesting in his inability to decide. He let out a grunt. It was only a jacket after all.

"The green."

His valet nodded and helped him into it, then hurried off to re-hang the charcoal. Quintin tugged on his sleeves as he looked himself over in the mirror. Not too pompous, yet not too casual. He was dressed just right for a London season. But after a morning like the one he'd had, he felt certain he'd be more comfortable in nothing but his shirtsleeves and a vest. Too bad such would be quite unseemly.

Then again, he wasn't planning on going out.

No. He shook his head and headed for the bedchamber door. He'd have to remain sensible so long as he'd changed his mind and decided to stay in London. He passed more than one maid on his way down the stairs. They all seemed to glance at him with the same wary look. After decreeing that he was removing himself that same day, and then only hours later reversing his decision, he figured the household had rather a good reason to be viewing him with concern.

Oh, blast. Quintin's step paused and he placed a hand against the bridge of his nose. He would need to write Lord Dunn. *Again.* He'd already written to the man that morning explaining the necessity of postponing their meeting. He'd simply stated that he felt he could no longer stay away from his estate, leaving Esther fully out of it. Lord Dunn had already written back, stating he fully understood and that perhaps he could make the journey out to Cottonhold and meet with him there.

Quintin shook his head; Esther had been right. There *were* men who were willing to help him, if only he spoke up. Only now, what would Lord Dunn think when Quintin wrote him and told of his change in plans? No doubt the man would think him fickle and undependable. Quintin let out a loud sigh. But what else could he do? He couldn't explain about Esther. He'd have to find some other reason to justify his staying.

No doubt Venetia would need a full explanation. At least she knew enough about Esther—or had gathered enough as of late—that he didn't need to feel bad about admitting anything. Quintin glanced down the hallway. She was probably in the parlor right now. She usually read by the large window so that she might watch the carriages roll by. But he could talk to her later. He turned toward the study door.

He paused again, not two steps later. If he delayed speaking with Venetia, he very well might risk making her even *more* angry at him. Quintin shook his head at himself, then caught a young maid watching him from down the hall where she was standing with a duster in hand. She didn't speak to Quintin, but the look on her face told him she wasn't at all sure he was in his right mind.

Quintin suppressed a dark chuckle which threatened to slip out. There was absolutely nothing humorous about his morning talk with Esther, nor his current situation. Gads, he wasn't even sure what to make of all Esther had told him.

Turning on his heel, he made his way toward the parlor. He'd best get this over with so he could focus on what he was going to do next. After his immediate anger at that blackguard, Fallow, and even at Esther's parents had subsided, he realized he still wasn't sure how to proceed.

Voices drifted out the open door to the parlor. And not just one voice, but two. Who was visiting with Venetia? She hadn't made her bows yet and Penelope wasn't here, so she hadn't had any visitors so far this Season. None that Quintin knew of, anyway.

"Then, of course," the visitor said in a clearly female voice, "I told my dear sister that she really had to stop worrying so. My nephew was going to be fine and well again soon enough. And so he was. Not two weeks later he was up and climbing that tree again."

Quintin knew, even before entering the room and seeing her face, who was visiting. He entered quietly enough that neither woman looked up, and he took to standing just behind Venetia's chair.

"I was quite glad to see it. I had worried my well wishes were misplaced. But Heather frets so sometimes and I feel it is my duty as her sister to help her through those moments."

Lady Christina, who sat across from Venetia, didn't even seem to notice that he'd entered. Father had more than once impressed upon him that it was his duty to let ladies know when he'd entered a room, so that they did not feel spied upon. He'd always felt the act a bit pointless. If they didn't care to notice when he entered to begin with, why force them into it? As he'd grown, he'd come to acknowledge that it was what society expected of him. Still, there were times he was far more content to rather remain hidden from those visiting, much like Tom Thumb. Of course, he would rather *not* be swallowed by a cow or try to battle giants.

"You have a sister as well, I understand. Do you not feel the same? I must say that I feel quite certain that is part of my duty as a sister to lift Heather when she is downcast."

Finally, with Father's firm expression looming before Quintin's mind, Quintin felt he couldn't let her go on longer; he let out a small *ahem* to draw attention to himself.

Lady Christina's words stopped abruptly, and she glanced up his way. Her cheeks pinkened a bit and she smiled.

"Good day to you both," Quintin said.

Venetia turned about in her chair and looked up at him as well. "Good day to you." Though the words were common enough, the look she gave him was a mix of curiosity and frustration.

Well, there was no denying he'd justly earned both from her. Moving around the small sitting area, he chose a chair close to his sister, but not too far from Lady Christina as to be misconstrued as being rude.

"I had heard your sister was staying with you. Keeping house, I believe?" Lady Christina—bless her heart—didn't give Venetia a moment to ask even a vague, roundabout question regarding his upheaval of the house that morning. "I thought I must come by and visit. We've been having a splendid time of it, too. So much better than the other night you and I spent at the Monstattens'. That really was not such a grand supper party as I had hoped, after all. But then, my cousin is a bit of a wild one at times. Anyway, your sister and I were just discussing the cotton dresses which are really becoming quite popular now."

Oh, drat, as Esther would say. Cotton dresses? Well, he'd be a gentleman and listen regardless. Lady Christina continued her soliloquy with very little input from either him or Venetia. Still, he nodded and hummed in all the right places, though his mind was far away from anything she said.

Esther's face, the tears running down her cheeks, every word she'd spoken, it all took up his entire concentration. He ran her story through his mind over and over again. No matter his effort, he still couldn't make heads or tails of it.

He understood what she'd done and why. While he hurt for Lady Helen and her situation, he also couldn't find it in himself to blame or be upset at Esther.

"Do you enjoy horseback riding, Lord Quintin?" Lady Christina asked, jumping the conversation from laces to horses with no apparent bridge.

"Yes, quite," he responded.

Lady Christina smiled and continued on about how she did so enjoy taking a turn on her small mare. And then on to how her brother used to ride at the most neck-breaking speed and how terrified it made their mother.

The real problems was, Esther *did* blame herself. So much so that she had decided to punish herself for what she'd done. He'd noticed the change in her, only he'd not been able to define it so well until now. She'd not only pulled away from him, she'd began to pull away from life.

"We have several beautiful family portraits of us as children, do we not, Quintin?" Venetia asked, Lady Christina having guided the conversation from horses to sitting for portraits in less than four sentences.

He crossed his legs. "Quite so. Most though are at Ramport Manor."

"I have heard many wonderful things regarding Ramport Manor," Lady Christina said. "I do miss the country life when I spend so much time in London. There's something about the constant crush here that just exhausts me."

Esther didn't speak as much as she once had. She didn't seem to smile quite as much either. They were small changes. Nothing grand. It wasn't as though she'd suddenly taken to avoiding society and frowning all day long. Still, Quintin felt certain, deep inside, that her wanting to continue a closer acquaintance with him was not the only casualty of India.

If it *had* been the only casualty—if she had changed in no other way save her regard toward him—would he still have decided to stay in London?

"Well, I must be off. I have more calls to make today." Lady Christina stood.

"It was very thoughtful of you to come visit me," Venetia said. There was more than a hint of sincerity in Venetia's statement. Had she been lonelier than he'd realized staying here in London with him? He'd asked her more than once if she was, and she'd always denied it.

He stood and spoke the expected farewell as Lady Christina left.

In the suddenly silent room, Venetia turned on him, studying him with an intense look.

"I can explain," he started.

"You'd better. First I'm awakened by a maid hurrying about my room saying you've decided we were leaving before supper. As I'm hurrying about getting things packed, I am informed—not by *you* but by yet a different maid—that you've changed your mind and we are to stay. Then, Lady Christina shows up nearly in tears over something that happened at the Monstattens' and how you've been ignoring her ever since."

The last bit caught Quintin quite off guard. "Excuse me?"

"Do you like her?"

"What?"

"Do you like her?" Venetia stated each word clearly and clipped, as though he'd lacked the basic knowledge necessary to grasp her simple question.

No one had ever asked him that before—not about any lady. His family had somehow, over the years, figured out his prefer- ence for Esther. There hadn't been anyone to ask *about* after he'd lost his heart to Esther, with her deep brown eyes and many smiles.

"Well?"

Quintin shook his head. "You know I don't." He turned around and stalked over toward the sitting area. Blast it all. If he was having to remind *anyone* that his heart was still all Esther's, then his situation was worse off than he thought. He kicked back into the chair he'd occupied before and slouched heavily.

Venetia followed him, sitting gently in her chair. "She never came right out and said it, but I got the very distinct impression she was concerned your regard for her was greatly diminished because her performance was less than perfect."

"That's absurd." He would never think less of Lady Christina, or anyone, for having stumbled through a piece a bit.

"You may think so, but Lady Christina clearly doesn't," Venetia said. "Her performances mean a lot to her. She works hard and she puts a lot of herself into her music."

"I hadn't realized I'd been ignoring her." He shrugged with one shoulder. "I think we simply haven't been to the same gatherings since that night." He'd been too wrapped up in worrying over Esther. He should have been more sensitive.

Lud. If Lady Christina was upset because he'd supposedly been ignoring her, that meant she was beginning to think they might have a connection. He glanced up toward the ceiling. When had life gotten so turned around?

"She was still upset regarding Lord Copeland's comments, was she?" he asked.

Esther was still upset regarding India.

"Most certainly," Venetia said, picking up a bit of needlepoint.

Quintin leaned his elbow against the armrest and faced Venetia fully. "Why."

"Pardon me?" she asked, pulling her needle through the fabric.

"Why *still* be upset?"

She lowered her embroidery hoop. "It sounds to me like Lord Copeland was excessively rude."

He had been, but that wasn't what Quintin needed to understand. "So why not get mad at him? He is her cousin, after all. Why come to me about it?"

Venetia listed her head, watching him. "I suppose she's worried you'll always remember her as having fallen short."

"But I won't."

"True. But she doesn't know you well enough to realize that."

"Just imagine," he said, leaning in yet further, "that she *did* know me well enough to know I wouldn't care. Yet, she held on to her worry anyway. What would you make of that?"

Most certainly Esther would not appreciate him telling anyone of her experience in India, so this would have to be good enough.

Venetia thought for a moment, lifting the needlepoint back up and adding two more stitches. "I would say the young woman probably remembers she's fallen short whenever she sees you. I'd say the young woman probably feels what she has done is part of who she is now."

Quintin slowly leaned back in his chair. Part of who she is now. That was it. Esther not only felt bad over what she'd done, she felt it was part of the woman she had become.

That he could wrap his head around. It made sense now why she refused to allow him to court her, why she smiled less, and why she seemed less full of joy.

Quintin stood. "Thank you."

Venetia only smiled at the thread and fabric in her hands.

He strode toward the parlor door. He knew now—finally—why Esther was behaving as she was. He finally understood what he was up against. All he needed to do now was help Esther understand that what she'd *done* wasn't part of who she *was*. It probably wouldn't be easy; he wasn't even sure he could explain it if she let him. But at least he could see the problem clearly.

"Quintin," Venetia called just before he moved out of the room. "I'm glad you're not giving up on Esther."

How had she—? Quintin leaned a hand against the doorway. It didn't matter. "Sometimes I wonder if you aren't far more grown up than any of us give you credit."

Venetia laughed easily. "I don't wonder at all. I, for one, am quite sure of it."

CHAPTER 17

*J*oan was humming. Esther, sitting before a mirror, followed Joan with her eyes through the reflection. She was still quite overwrought herself after her conversation with Quintin three mornings ago. Nonetheless, she was finding Joan's blatant infatuation quite diverting. The abigail brought over a light pink dress and held it up for Esther to approve.

"I'm thinking this one, with that long strand of beads you look so good in," Joan said.

"That would look lovely."

Joan turned away, off to fetch the rest of Esther's things. The humming began again. Joan returned and combed out Esther's hair. The brush moved in slow, fluid motions. Gracious, when Esther first thought Joan and Will would rub together well, she'd never imagined this. The dear young woman was quite taken, it would seem.

"Do you have any plans for tonight?" Esther asked.

Joan instantly blushed. "Perhaps."

"Well?" Esther wasn't about to let Joan off without hearing the whole of it.

Joan's face broke into a wide smile and she sighed. "Will Stanley has been to call on me every evening this week."

Esther spun around in her chair. "Has he?" That was exciting news.

Joan nodded. "He mentioned maybe going for a walk tonight."

"That will be magical." Esther faced the mirror once more.

Joan sighed again and returned to Esther's hair. "He has been quite attentive ever since we chanced upon one another at your coming-out ball."

Esther tried hard to suppress the smile that was threatening to break out across her own face. It seemed she'd done what she'd set out to do. Will and Joan could handle it from here. "I'm very pleased to hear that."

"Granted," Joan continued, putting down the brush and twisting locks of Esther's hair to pin atop her head, "he is very busy at Dunn's. He hasn't said as much, but I think after he calls on me, he has to return and work late into the night."

"He must seriously be interested in you, then, if he's willing to set aside so much time for you."

"Do you really think so, miss?" Joan paused, a bit of Esther's hair in her hands.

"Yes, I do." And she meant it. "I would not say so if I believed otherwise." Will seemed quite an upstanding sort of man. Esther was pleased the two were getting along.

"I'm hopeful that you are right."

Joan quickly finished Esther's hair. Soon, she was humming once more. If all went as well as they both hoped, Esther would be needing a new abigail soon. To think, she may have had a hand in another woman's happiness. It was a very pleasant thought indeed.

With her hair done, Joan helped Esther into her dress. Esther was ready for the opera and waiting near the front door in no time at all. Truthfully, Esther would have much rather stayed at home tonight, but Mother would not hear a word of it.

"Now dear," Mother said as they and Father climbed into the carriage, "Lord Copeland is rumored to be in attendance tonight.

He's been paying you quite a bit of attention as of late. I think if you only show a bit more affection you will secure him quickly enough."

Esther's stomach flipped. "Secure him?"

"Preferably before London grows too hot," Mother said, fanning herself. "Don't let this unusually cool spring fool you. Summer will be blistering."

Secure Lord Copeland? Something about hearing Mother say as much out loud made it all feel very real. More than that, it made Esther realize just how much of her own wishes Mother was wholly unaware of. Mother actually thought Esther *wanted* a connection with Lord Copeland. Then again, Mother hadn't cared either way when they were in India. So long as Mother had the society she craved, she seemed to have stopped seeing anything else.

"I thought you would prefer to stay in London until Christmas."

Mother didn't respond and they rode to the opera in silence.

Esther stepped out of the carriage and looked up at the grand building before her. In that moment, it seemed massive. Oppressive. Mother took hold of her elbow and led her inside. Could she really do this? Secure Lord Copeland? Her supper threatened to make itself known the more she thought about it. But what about Quintin?

She'd told him emphatically a few days before that she could never marry him. She still felt that way. After all she'd done and become, she couldn't see herself with him. Every day she'd be reminded that she hadn't become the woman she'd wanted to be as a child. It was best she cut all ties with her past—her *entire* past—and start again.

With Copeland?

The idea would not sit well with her.

Esther was not the least bit surprised when, not only did Lord Copeland show up at her family's box during the intermission, but Mother insisted he stay and sit with them for the remainder of the performance. Esther kept her hands demurely in her lap—twisting around one another though they were—and away from where Lord Copeland may try to take one and hold it.

He might be her future. This might be the man she wed and spent the rest of her life with. But she couldn't do it. Not tonight. Not after seeing Joan so happy about Will and with thoughts of Quintin ever swirling before her eyes.

A pair of men on stage, placed in the story with the only purpose of making the audience laugh, chased one another with exaggerated expressions and vases held high above their heads. Lord Copeland didn't so much as chuckle but remained ever stern and drab. As the two men exited the stage and the heroine entered once more, Lord Copeland leaned closer to Esther.

His nearness sent bits of icy irritation down her arm. She stood abruptly. Lord Copeland's gaze, as well as that of her parents, shot to her.

"Pardon me," she said, realizing what a forward thing she'd just done. "I only need to stretch my legs a bit. I'll not leave the box." She strode past them all and toward the curtain separating their box from the hallway beyond.

Behind her, Lord Copeland leaned forward. Did he mean to follow her? Oh, she prayed he wouldn't. She only needed some space and time to think.

"Do not worry," Mother leaned forward, engaging Lord Copeland in a soft conversation. "She has always had the hardest time sitting still for very long. She is my own daughter and yet I cannot deny it."

Blessedly, Lord Copeland remained in his seat and returned to blandly watching the opera unfold. Esther slowly paced back and forth, careful that her steps not make a sound and disrupt anyone. She would have to make a decision regarding Lord Copeland soon.

Someone whispered her name.

Esther turned around. Lord Copeland and her parents were all still facing forward, eyes on the stage. There was no one else in the box.

"Esther."

The voice had come from the curtain. Esther slipped up close to where it met the wall. "Quintin?"

She could hear him chuckle softly. "I figured you wouldn't be able to stay seated for the entirety."

He knew her too well. "You can't come in. If you move the curtain, at all the light will shine directly on Mother." Though she'd been quite terrified of this moment—speaking with him again after their previous conversation—knowing he was right there beside her brought more relief than guilt. It also caused her to smile.

"I tried to get here before intermission ended."

"Too long primping before the mirror?" she teased. It felt so good to be speaking with him, as friends, again. It had only been three days but she'd desperately missed it.

"I wish. No, my man of business paid me an unexpected visit today."

Judging by his tone, it hadn't been a pleasant visit either. "Is everything all right at Cottonhold?" The soft echoes of wanting to reach out to him pulsed against her. Drat, she'd truly, deeply missed him these past few days.

"The house is still standing. Other than that, I can't say much for it."

"Tell me." It was nice to speak on something other than herself.

He grumbled softly. "It seems not one of the tenants knows how to make a profit. I have a sheep farmer whose sheep keep dying. I have another farmer who planted his crop too early. Today I learned that the vicar has decided to holiday for the entire summer and expects me to find a temporary replacement."

"You could always stand up and sermonize yourself."

Quintin chuckled at that. "I think I would be hanged for single-handedly causing more people to stop attending church than any other man in all England."

"I would come and listen."

"Until you couldn't tolerate sitting any longer."

"Then I'd pace in the back and listen. If no other patrons were present it wouldn't be as though I'd be bothering anyone."

She'd expected him to laugh again. Instead, her comment was met with only silence. With the heavy curtain between them, she couldn't see him at all. Was he smiling? Frowning? Slouching? What did his eyes look like right now? She imagined pushing a bit of his hair across his forehead so that she could better see his blue eyes. Heat rushed over her at the thought.

His voice came much softer this time. "Esther, I'm afraid I'm failing."

"Oh no, Quintin. Don't talk like that."

"I can't seem to make my deuced estate turn a profit. Truth is, I couldn't support you even if . . ."

She reached around the curtain. She didn't dare pull it aside enough for her to actually *see* him, but she could slip her hand through without drawing her parent's attention. Her fingers wiggled in the air. Quintin's hand took hold of hers. Warmth spread from her palm, up her arm, and into her chest.

They hadn't held hands since they were children. They'd both grown and changed since then. His hand certainly wasn't the hand of a boy's any longer. Yet, it was so very familiar all the same. It was the hand of Quintin—*her* Quintin.

"You are not a failure, Quintin Lockhart."

"The money books certainly say I am."

"You have stupid tenants, that's all."

He did laugh at that. "My man of business keeps saying I should reassign the land to new farmers."

"What do you think you should do?"

"I don't know." His words came faster. "I know these people. I've held their children and worked beside them. I've brought them Christmas baskets every winter for four years. I've seen to it that they have enough coal in the winter and enough water in the summer." There was a pause. "I can't turn my back on them now."

"Then don't. You'll find a way to make it all work."

"I don't see how. Nothing I've tried thus far has made any kind of a difference."

She gave his hand a squeeze. "You're a smart man, Quintin."

"Are you saying I should believe in myself even when I haven't measured up to my own expectations thus far?"

"Yes. I—" What Quintin was actually saying hit Esther. She gave his hand a frustrated tug. "Don't turn this back on me now. We were having such a lovely conversation."

"Lovely? I just admitted to being a complete failure."

At least they hadn't been talking about her and her failures.

There was the rustle of fabric and when Quintin spoke next, she could tell his voice came from directly next to the curtain. "If you don't want to marry me, Esther, that is all right. But you cannot continue to blame yourself for what happened in India." At his words, sharp tears formed in her eyes. Her chest tightened and she found it hard to breathe. "You are not what you did then; you are considerate, optimistic, and a wonderful woman."

Esther shook her head, and her forehead bumped softly against the fabric.

"Don't shake your head," Quintin said, a bit of laughter in his tone. "I'm not exaggerating. You did one thing that you regret. That doesn't make *all* of you bad."

Esther brushed at her cheeks. Her long, silk gloves came away wet at the fingertips. "You best leave, before my father or Lord Copeland realizes you're here."

Quintin didn't release her hand. "Why are you even entertaining his attentions?"

"I have to marry someone. I have not the means to support myself."

"But you must know he would never make you happy."

Her jaw tightened. "That's the point," she said, struggling to keep her voice quiet.

"Esther, please, I don't—"

"It's like I told you before. I don't deserve love." And she wouldn't risk hurting someone else by marrying a man she loved, only to disappoint him later when he realized just what kind of a woman she truly was.

"Of course you deserve love." His voice was so soft.

It made the tears swell all the faster. She blinked, trying to clear her vision. She *could not* cry here, at the opera. Everyone would know.

Quintin's voice came again. "When was the last time you pulled out your watercolors?"

How had he guessed?

"Esther, making yourself miserable will not fix—"

Esther tugged against Quintin's hand; she couldn't do this right now, couldn't face her own horrid nature. He released her. "Good night, Quintin."

Esther turned her back on him, only to find her parents and Lord Copeland standing and moving her direction. Her heart leapt painfully against her chest. Had they caught her and Quintin's whispered conversation? Not one of them seemed displeased. Glancing past them, Esther could see the rest of the audience also standing and moving about. She'd not even noticed that the opera had ended.

Lord Copeland strode purposely over toward her. "How did you enjoy the last act?"

"Oh, Esther, dear," Mother said, close on Lord Copeland's heels. "Are you crying? Really, I did not think the performance all *that* moving."

"Do not blame her," Lord Copeland said, taking her hand and patting it. Esther suddenly felt quite like he viewed her as only a child. "She no doubt felt deeply for the heroine."

"Yes," Esther stumbled a bit around the words. She couldn't for the life of her remember how this opera was supposed to end. But playing along with Lord Copeland's excuse was better than explaining the truth. "Yes, that is all, Mother."

"Well," Lady Harrington said. "I suppose I shan't take you to any more performances where the heroine dies. What will everyone think when they see your pink eyes?"

The heroine died? Oh dear. She really had missed the entire ending. So long as no one knew about her speaking with Quintin, she supposed it didn't matter.

"Come." Lord Copeland stepped past her and threw open the curtain. Esther caught her breath; what would he and her parents say to finding Quintin hovering about their box? But Lord Copeland continued as though nothing was amiss. "We shall get you some refreshments and speak no more of pointless notions like dying for love."

He strode out into the hallway, clearly expecting them all to follow. Esther tentatively moved out of the box. The brilliant light of the hallway temporarily forced her to squint. Blinking, she searched the ever-growing crush spilling out into the hall.

Quintin was nowhere to be seen.

CHAPTER 18

*Q*uintin took a sip of port and then rested his cup back onto the table. Leaning back, and resisting the urge to fully slump, he let his gaze wander to the ceiling above. Gentlemen talked and moved about him. White's was busier than normal today. It brought to mind the book he'd most recently reread, *Ivanhoe*. The gentlemen about him, though dressed quite differently, did behave how he'd imagined the crusaders would act after returning home from a long journey. Joyful, full of drink, and equally as full of self-importance.

Placing his own cup back on the low table before him, Quintin picked up the small sheet of paper he'd been taking notes on. His conversation with Lord Dunn had left him much to mull over. Blessedly, Lord Dunn hadn't pried into why Quintin had wanted to leave so quickly, and then equally as fast changed his mind and stayed in London. Moreover, he'd still been willing to meet with Quintin. Their conversation had been long and detailed.

Quintin slipped the page of notes into his jacket pocket. The earl had agreed with John, in that some of his land ought to be reassigned to new farmers. He didn't press the point as hard as John had yesterday, though. Still, the idea didn't sit right with Quintin.

He could always sell part of the estate. The surge of income would be a temporary boon and allow him to more fully invest in the land he kept. Then, over time, he could possibly expand Cottonhold back to its current size.

Quintin shut his eyes and let his chin rock forward onto his chest. It felt like a loser's tactic, though. Not something a man did when he expected to proudly pass the estate down onto his son one day, and then onto his grandson, and his great-grandson. Not that he was likely to have any sons, since the only woman he'd ever loved seemed set against him.

Still, he had enjoyed their conversation last night. It had brought to mind stories of Sherwood Forest and one particular bandit once rumored to live there. He too had had to sneak about and steal moments with his lovely Maid Mary. Or, so the stories went.

"Lord Quintin."

He opened his eyes and looked up. Lord Harrington scowled down at him.

"May I join you?" the man asked, his tone brisk.

"Yes, of course." Quintin had only spoken with Esther's father on a handful of occasions. The man hadn't cared for children when Quintin was young, and they hadn't had cause to speak with one another much since.

"Is there anything I can do for you, Lord Harrington?"

"Yes." He said, each word forcibly punched out. "You can stay away from my daughter."

"Excuse me, sir?"

Lord Harrington rested his elbow against one knee and leaned in close toward Quintin. "Don't think for a moment that I've been blind to what you've been up to."

"I'm sorry. But I don't quite—"

"Sneaking out after her during her coming-out ball. Always showing up at the same gatherings as us. Then last night, at the opera. I know you two were talking."

Quintin felt all the air leave his lungs. How had he allowed things to fall apart so completely? Then again, with the way his entire life was going, he was a fool for not seeing this coming.

"I promise you, nothing untoward has happened."

"I don't care. Society will think it has, and Esther will face its wrath."

Quintin shook his head. He wouldn't let that happen.

"Listen, boy, I know you two used to be friends. I was surprised but pleased when we first arrived in London and you showed no signs of wanting to court my daughter."

Because Esther wouldn't allow him to openly court her.

"But you still haven't fully left her alone. You keep following her around, always in the background."

Quintin felt a bit of his own anger smolder in his chest.

"Did you think I wouldn't see through your plan? Everyone knows Cottonhold is struggling. But I was willing to give you the benefit of the doubt. I was willing to believe that it was below a Lockhart to snare a woman for her dowry."

Quintin ground his jaw; that was preposterous. His hand clenched, and he leaned forward.

Before he could say anything, Lord Harrington spoke on, his voice low. "Let me make myself clear. You are to stay away from my daughter." Without giving Quintin time to respond, he stood and strode away.

Quintin covered his face and muffled his frustrated growl against his palms. How dare Lord Harrington accuse him of such. It was utter rot. If Esther wanted Quintin to court her, they should be allowed to. If Esther didn't want that, then he would respect her wishes. It was as simple as that. Her dowry had *nothing* to do with it.

First India, and their disregard for her safety there, and now this? Quintin stood abruptly and quickly strode out of White's, fuming the entire way back to Ramport House. This was ridiculous. Wholly ridiculous.

Quintin yanked the front door open. John stood just inside.

"What do you want?" Quintin barked.

"Sir, it's time you return to Cottonhold."

Quintin was about to disagree, but there was something different about John. He wasn't so upset. He wasn't seething and demanding Quintin return. There was a stillness about him and a hollowness to his words. It made Quintin far more nervous than any of his previous blustering.

"What's happened?" Quintin asked, afraid to hear the answer.

"You best get your household packing up first. I'll wait in the book room." The man turned and began making his way, almost dragging himself, up the stairs.

"It's that bad?" Quintin asked.

John nodded, his head slowly moving up and down. "It's that bad."

CHAPTER 19

*E*sther glanced about the room. Almack's was full tonight, so perhaps she just couldn't *find* Quintin was all. He very well could still be here, even if she hadn't seen him all evening.

Lord Copeland took hold of her hand, pulling her toward him and her mind back to the dance they were in the middle of.

"You look dazzling this evening," he said as he passed by her, his voice as flat and unaffected as ever.

"Thank you, sir," she muttered, but too late for him to hear most likely. Esther took advantage of the next turn the dance required to look along the far wall. Quintin was not there either.

She met Lord Copeland again in the center of the room and smiled up at him. With any luck, he wouldn't realize just how distracted she was tonight. It wasn't as though it was his fault. She just couldn't get her last conversation with Quintin out of her head.

Lord Copeland smiled down at her as well, and they took hands as they moved forward in a line with another couple. Ironically, when last they were out together, at the opera, she had also been struggling with keeping her last conversation with Quintin out of her head. They may have grown, and they may have changed, but that one fact remained the same. Her moments with Quintin were the ones she thought back on the most. The ones she pined for the most. The ones she loved the most.

The set ended and Lord Copeland escorted Esther back to her Mother. With a polite bow, he promised to return for her come the midnight dance. Esther only nodded, wishing he would leave already so she could be alone and think.

Had Quintin been right? He'd said that just because she'd done one bad thing didn't make her bad on the whole. She wasn't fully sure she agreed. When an apple had a spot of mold, one tossed it away. When a vase cracked on one side, it was replaced. Moreover, what she'd done hadn't been small. It hadn't been a wrong note during a performance. It hadn't been a moment of embarrassment during a ball or supper party.

She'd ruined another woman's life. Forced her into an unwanted marriage.

Then again, Quintin's insistence wouldn't leave her. She wanted to believe he was right. Wanted to think that her one wrong misstep did not make her wholly bad.

Two of Mother's friends came and joined them. Esther sat up straighter. Perhaps she could try, just for tonight, to pretend she wasn't an awful person. See where it led.

The conversation was predictable, but still diverting. They talked of the young ladies of the season and who was being seriously courted by whom. They talked lengths of sleeves and lace and the new cotton dresses which were beginning to gain popularity.

"Oh good," Lady Williamson said softly, sitting to Esther's right.

"Pardon me?" Esther asked, turning toward the lady more fully.

Lady Williamson nodded subtly toward a thin young woman only a few paces away. "It seems Miss Rebecca has avoided her father's schemes well enough."

She searched the face of the young woman; Esther knew she'd seen the woman before. "I'm afraid I don't follow."

"Miss Rebecca's father had planned on the young woman

marrying a certain man of status and wealth. But the man was a scoundrel, and everyone knew it. Still, her father pressed her toward him. I am glad Miss Rebecca has made her own preference known."

Remembrance dawned. This was the slender woman she'd stood beside while dancing with Copeland, moments before she'd seen Quintin for the first time this Season. She'd wondered at the time if Miss Rebecca knew the type of man she was dancing with. Apparently, she had. "Is the man she's dancing with now any better?"

"Lord Hughes? Oh yes, far better a man, if less well-off."

Esther didn't want to allow her mind to float away from Miss Rebecca and drift back to Lady Helen. Miss Rebecca had been able to have a say in her future partner. Lady Helen hadn't been given such a choice.

"Take it from an old lady," the matron to Esther's left continued. "Marrying for convenience has its place. I won't deny that. Goodness knows my own marriage was such as one." Her voice grew sorrowful. "But so was my sister's. Only she didn't end up as lucky as I. Died young, poor soul, all the life stripped out of her by the blackguard she married."

Esther started slightly at the vulgar term coming from a woman of class and distinction. Still, perhaps there wasn't any better way to say it. Is that what would happen to Lady Helen?

"Lady Esther, how nice to see you again."

Esther glanced up. Lady Christina stood before her, dressed in lavender and soft blue. "Good evening."

"Would you take a turn about the room with me?"

Why did Lady Christina want to speak with her? She stood and linked arms with the woman. Was this about Quintin? Why else would Lady Christina seek her out?

As Esther expected, Lady Christina lost no time in filling the space between them with words. She spoke of getting ready for the ball that evening, and how none of her dresses seemed just right. Then, in only a few words, she catapulted the conversation on to

Bath and the many diversions to be had there. That was quickly left for Lady Christina's thoughts on Lady Trulow's newly decorated parlor.

Esther nodded, and slipped in a thought here or there. Was Lady Christina trying to befriend her in the hopes that Quintin would see her more favorably? No doubt it hadn't slipped her attention that Esther and he were good friends. Or, they had been. Esther wasn't sure what they were now. The way he'd confided in her the other day at the opera certainly made her feel like they were good friends. But the way he'd held her hand as he did it spoke of something more. Quintin wanted that something more. He'd never tried to hide that from her.

Nonetheless, whenever she imagined herself reaching out to him, accepting his attentions, painful panic filled her chest and she could hardly breathe. What right did she have to accept such a man's suit when she'd been the cause of so much pain to another?

"Lady Esther, did you hear me?"

Esther's head came up and she faced Lady Christina. Judging by the look on the other woman's face she'd missed something important in their conversation.

"I'm sorry," Esther said. "I'm afraid I was woolgathering."

"I said"—her words came out clipped; apparently, Lady Christina was not pleased to learn Esther wasn't fully paying attention—"you will explain things to him for me, will you not?"

"Explain . . .?"

Lady Christina pursed her lips. "To Lord Quintin. Explain why, in his absence, I . . ." Some of her bravado died. "I plan to accept another's suit."

Now she *did* have Esther's full attention. "And you want me to explain as much to Lord Quintin?"

"You two are quite close, I know." Lady Christina had taken to shifting from one foot to another, almost as though she were uncomfortable with the conversation she herself had started. "You do think he'll understand, won't he? After the scandal regarding his estate and all—"

"Scandal?"

Lady Christina placed hands on hips. "Men may look down on lady's gossip, but truthfully how else is a woman to know the details she needs to make a smart alliance? Yes, scandal. It may not have hit the papers yet, but I wager it will soon."

"What happened?"

"Well." Lady Christina leaned in. Her eagerness to relay what she'd heard only made Esther feel all the more ill. "Apparently, one of his tenants pulled the wool over his eyes. Claimed he needed more seed than he could afford—something about a crop going bad after being planted too early. So Lord Quintin offered to front the cost of new seed. But his crops were fine. The farmer took the new seed and *sold it* himself to another farmer a county over."

Oh, drat.

"I suppose I should take it as a compliment."

"How so?" Esther tried to keep her tone soft and congenial. Though, she could not for the life of her figure out how such an incident would be a compliment to Lady Christina. Esther herself was feeling quite furious on Quintin's behalf.

"The rumors among the servants is that the farmer only got away with it because Lord Quintin was too wrapped up here in London to go and inspect the crop himself." Lady Christina leaned in a bit. "Too wrapped with *a lady*." She smoothed her skirt. "It's all just rumors, of course. No one seems to know the particulars."

Well, for not knowing the particulars, Lady Christina was certainly willing to spread the rumor. Esther needed to speak with Quintin, learn for herself how bad his situation was. Perhaps there was something she could do to help? She couldn't imagine what, but still, she needed to ask. A quick word from Lady Christina's earlier sentence resurfaced. "Did you say, 'in his absence'?"

"Oh yes. " Lady Christina's head bobbed. "Had you not even heard he'd left town?"

Quintin was no longer in London? Esther slowly shook her head.

"Huh." Lady Christina shrugged. "I suppose I was wrong in

assuming you were close friends." She shrugged again, as though she hadn't just greatly hurt Esther. "Yes, he's returned to Cottonhold, of course. I suppose he'll try to salvage what he can of his reputation and the estate. If I were him, I'd seriously consider selling and giving up on the whole venture. Society may never forget if he stays master of that place. At least if he were to sell, his name would eventually stop being connected with *the Cottonhold scandal*." She said the last bit as though she were discussing something humorous and diverting. Not at all like she was discussing the livelihood of a man whom, until tonight, she had most certainly had designs on.

What kind of woman turned her back on a man for being too kind and generous? Helping a struggling tenant was just the sort of thing Quintin would do. His only flaw was in staying in London too long, when his estate needed him. Staying in the hopes that she, Esther, would willingly accept his hand. Instead of feeling flattered at the idea, Esther only felt guilty.

CHAPTER 20

Quintin pushed the ledger toward Lord Dunn. "Any suggestions you have, I'm willing to hear." He still couldn't believe that Lord Dunn had agreed to come to Cottonhold to help.

Lord Dunn pulled out a pair of small spectacles and rested them atop his nose. "I'm not saying I have all the answers," he said, taking hold of the ledger, "but I'm willing to assist where I can."

Quintin sat in silence, waiting. Coming home to Cottonhold had brought a mix of emotions. A good deal of him was happy, even relieved, to be home once more. He'd missed the familiar surroundings, especially his books.

However, he'd come home without Esther, and that had left a hole inside of him that still ached and throbbed.

Lord Dunn leaned in, pointing out a line in the ledger. The earl asked a few questions about last year's grain, which Quintin was glad he could answer fully. The conversation rolled into one on buying and selling and leveraging the market to its fullest.

Quintin nodded and listened and even took notes. To think, he'd almost not agreed to have Lord Dunn come out at all. After the news about Coleston's betrayal, Quintin rather thought the earl would brand Quintin a fool and have nothing more to do with him. Yet, only a few days later a letter had arrived from the earl requesting an invitation to visit.

Lord Dunn shut the ledger and leaned back in his chair. "With those few changes, I think you'll find a bit more breathing room."

"Thank you. I think they will help." Of course, much of the desire to make Cottonhold a success had lessened since he wasn't readying the place for a Lady Lockhart.

The door opened and a footman moved inside. "Supper is ready, my lord."

Quintin placed the ledger back inside his desk. "Shall we?"

"Quite so," Lord Dunn said, pulling himself to his feet with the help of a cane. Together they moved out and down the hall toward the dining room.

"When is that new sheep doctor coming?" Lord Dunn asked.

"Lord Briston wrote to him on my behalf." Another gentleman who had surprised Quintin with his willingness to help. "He should be here early next week."

"Very good, very good."

They sat and were soon served. Lord Dunn said little during the first half of the meal, intent on his food.

Quintin pushed his food about his plate. He hadn't had much appetite since leaving London.

"You will need to replace a few of the tenants," Lord Dunn said suddenly and quite as though there had been no lull in the conversation. "I hear what you're saying about not wanting to, but I don't see any other way."

This was the one piece of the Cottonhold fix he was most loath to address. "As master here, those people are my responsibility. What kind of master am I if I turn those away who simply haven't learned yet what they need to know?" He himself was still learning how to be successful. It felt quite hypocritical to replace those who only lacked learning, same as he.

Lord Dunn pointed at Quintin with his fork. "What kind of a master would you be if you let a few bad apples spoil all the rest?"

Quintin bobbed his head back and forth; Lord Dunn had a point. He took a drink but didn't taste whatever was in his cup. "It still doesn't sit well with me." Replacing Henry wouldn't keep him up at nights. The farmer had already been sent off. "After we find a new tenant for Henry's land, I can only think of two others whom I can replace." They were both men without families, and who were less likely to show kindness and mercy to the others in the neighborhood. "But that is all; everyone else has families to support."

"Very well. I think that should be enough," Lord Dunn said, sitting back in his chair. "Now that I think of it, I know a man. I don't know why I didn't think of him before. He's quite skilled at finding the right sort of tenant. I've gone to him many a times for suggestions. Always has his ear to the ground, he does."

"Sounds like a talent I could benefit from."

"Most definitely, most definitely." Lord Dunn spooned some more potatoes into his mouth and chewed them quickly. "I'll write to him at once."

Quintin still could not understand why anyone would be willing to help him—he, the Lockhart son whom no one seemed to remember.

But Esther had been right. He was indebted to her. He'd only reached out to Briston and Dunn because she'd urged him to. Eventually he'd figured if she believed in him that much, perhaps he should try.

Now though, it was clear she didn't believe in him, not enough to trust him with her heart, anyway.

Would he ever get over her? It didn't seem very likely. Regardless, he was grateful she had pointed him toward these men; he *would* see Cottonhold a success. Then, perhaps when he was old and gray and more in need of a cane than even Dunn, it would be passed on to one of Felix and Jocelyn's sons. Or maybe someday Sheldon and Marianne would have a son and Quintin could find a way to pass it on to him?

"It was a lady, wasn't it?"

Quintin blinked—remembering that he had a guest sitting

directly across from him. "Excuse me?" He had a cup in his hand which he had also forgotten. He took another little sip and replaced it onto the table.

"You needing to rush off, and then deciding only hours later to stay." Lord Dunn shook his head. "It wasn't hard to figure out a lady was behind it all."

Quintin thought about denying it. Then again, what was the point? What happened in London had happened. Hiding it seemed trivial. It wouldn't bring Esther back. "Yes, but she chose something else."

"Some*thing* or some*one*?"

Quintin sat up straight once more and picked up his fork. "Does it matter?"

"Of course it matters. Another man you could fight. But, some notion of love or wealth or appearances is far harder to combat."

"It wasn't any of those." Quintin tried to eat but couldn't seem to make his fork do anything more than push his food around again.

"Well, whatever it was, I'm sorry to hear it. She's missing out on a fine gentleman in my opinion."

Quintin didn't want to discuss Esther any longer. Nor did he want to pretend he was interested in eating. He placed his fork back down and pushed his plate away. "Speaking of ladies, I do believe there was a very elegant widow sitting beside you that day we met in Hyde Park."

Lord Dunn's face broke out in a broad smile. "Ah, the lovely Mrs. Sarah Tompton." He leaned across the table a bit. "Don't tell anyone—Sarah wishes to speak with her children about it first—but I do believe you will have cause to congratulate me soon."

The news brought joy to Quintin. If anyone deserved a happy life with a woman who loved him, it was someone as generous as Dunn. But it also brought with it fresh ache in the form of a hard, unyielding longing for Esther.

Quintin tried his best to ignore the second emotion and picked up his glass. "Then let us toast to you and your good fortune."

Dunn picked up his own glass and clinked it against Quintin's. "May you also find such cause for happiness someday."

Quintin couldn't respond to that. Getting over Esther was going to take much time—probably every day until he died.

Dunn drained his glass and then scrapped his fork over his plate, picking up every last bit of food there. "I must say, when you do begin replacing a few tenants, make sure you don't replace your cook. She is a gem."

Of course she was. Quintin had hired her especially for Esther. But Esther wouldn't ever be living here. Quintin set his cup back on the table. Like so many other things, without Esther here, what did it matter?

CHAPTER 21

"*I* am glad you were able to join me so early this morning," Lord Copeland said from atop his black horse.

Esther shifted slightly in her sidesaddle. Though some women found it frightfully uncomfortable, Esther had found the strange seated position quite bearable, especially when it allowed her to ride Lily Bay on her own, instead of being pulled about in a carriage at another's discretion.

"I have some business at Westminster that I must see to later today," Lord Copeland continued. "You show quite a bit of sensibility agreeing to join me this morning instead of pouting that I couldn't take you out at the fashionable hour."

It was clear from his tone that calling someone 'sensible' was quite high praise in his opinion. Moreover, it was probably the best compliment he was ever likely to give her.

"It is a pleasant morning." Esther smiled as she looked about the trees around them in Hyde Park. What else *could* one say to such an almost-compliment? She wasn't by any means upset at riding out when there was still room to breathe the calm air of the park. At least now there was space for them to maneuver about. Only a few other couples were around.

"I felt the ball night before last was quite well attended," Lord Copeland said as their horses trotted at a comfortable, very proper gait, even if it was slower than Esther would have preferred.

"Yes, it was quite well attended." How was it that she and Lord Copeland had spent so many hours together, and yet had nothing better to say to one another than bland niceties? She missed the heartfelt conversations she and Quintin always shared. How was he fairing? As a woman with no formal connection to him, it wasn't as though Esther could write him a letter and ask. What she truly wanted was to spur Lily Bay forward and keep her at a run from here to Cottonhold. What wouldn't she give to speak with Quintin face to face, to hear his voice, and stand by him as he sorted through this difficulty?

"Will you be attending the Williamson's tonight?"

Esther forced her mind to stop wandering. "Perhaps. We have received a couple different invitations and I am not sure which my Mother chooses to accept for this evening." Esther was fairly sure that Mother *had* already accepted the Williamson's invitation, since Lady Williamson was one of mother's closest friends. But for now, Esther wasn't feeling up to encouraging Lord Copeland. She wasn't feeling up to much of anything beyond listening to the birds call and feeling Lily Bay's gentle rocking step beneath her.

"Lady Esther." The deep, male voice sent an unexpected chill right into her chest. "Well met. Well met indeed."

It couldn't be. No—that would be horrid.

But it was.

Esther watched, barely able to move enough to slow her mount, as Lieutenant Fallow and Lady Helen approached her, riding side by side in a small equipage. Esther felt lightheaded and clung tightly to Lily Bay's reins. She could not fall off. Then again, if she suddenly fell from her horse, she wouldn't have to spend much time speaking with Lieutenant Fallow. Perhaps it would be worth it.

"Hello," she finally managed to say.

While the lieutenant smiled up at her, quite at his ease, it appeared, his wife's gaze remained downward. "Of all the people I thought we'd pass today, you, Lady Esther, are not whom I expected."

Of all the people she had hoped to never see again, he was top on her list. Esther quickly introduced Lord Copeland to Lieutenant Fallow and his wife, Lady Helen. She wished that was all that would be required of her. However, once the formalities were done, it was quite obvious that Lieutenant Fallow wished to stay and talk for a moment.

Unsure of what else to say, but feeling everyone expected her to begin the conversation, Esther chose to simply state, "I had not heard you were returned from India, sir."

"Yes, not two weeks ago we arrived."

She should have known this day would come. Should have expected it. Had not his sole purpose in trying to capture a wife been so he could be reposted in England? Why had she not thought of this eventuality? Why had she allowed Lord Copeland to convince her it was a fine morning for a horse ride?

"I must say," Lieutenant Fallow continued, "England is even more lovely than I remembered it. Is it not, my dear?" He spoke the last bit to his wife. Though the sentence was clearly a question, the way he'd hesitated before the endearment almost made it sound as though he was asking if the term was acceptable, not only if Lady Helen enjoyed being home once more.

"As you say, Lieutenant Fallow." Lady Helen spoke barely above a whisper.

The lieutenant's face fell, but only for a moment. Then he was all smiles once again. "Yes, we are quite enjoying our return."

"Are you to be staying long then?" Mixed emotions swirled inside Esther; she desperately hoped never to see either of them again, yet at the same time if Lady Helen was more comfortable here in England than in India, Esther hoped she would be allowed to stay.

"Providence has smiled on us," Lieutenant Fallow said, "for I have been reassigned. We will be staying in England for the fore-seeable future."

"That is good news," Lord Copeland said. "No doubt Lady Helen is relieved to be back where life is more comfortable."

Lady Helen still did not look up. The matron's sad words from the other night echoed about Esther's head. It seemed quite possible that Lady Helen would die young, stripped of life because of the marriage she had been forced into.

After a moment of awkward silence, Lieutenant Fallow responded for her. "Most certainly, my wife is quite happy to be back home. Most of her family is here and she grew up not far from where we are residing now."

"How fortunate," Lord Copeland said, his tone light and easy. "It can be hard to be separated from one's family for years on end."

"Most certainly," Lieutenant Fallow agreed. If Esther wasn't mistaken, there was an undercurrent of sincerity which had been lacking in all his words up to that point.

They bid one another a good day, much to Esther's relief, and went their separate ways. Nonetheless, Lady Helen's gaunt expression wouldn't leave Esther. Had she appeared paler than when they'd been in India? Esther couldn't be sure.

"Did you see much of Lieutenant Fallow and his wife in India?" Lord Copeland asked.

"We were out much in the same society," Esther responded, not wanting to speak about or even think about her last conversation with the lieutenant.

"He seems pleasant enough. His wife, even more so."

"Because she was so quiet?"

"I would not say she was quiet—"

He wouldn't? Lady Helen had said no more than three words, and those were only to express her agreement with her husband.

"It is more that she is polite and demure. As ladies of rank are taught to be."

If that's how he felt, then Esther wasn't at all sure why he consistently sought out her company. But she didn't say as much.

She didn't say anything. Instead, Esther allowed Lord Copeland to speak on and on about the Fallows and their brief conversation without interrupting him. She suddenly had no desire for conversation. Perhaps she should fake yet another headache?

Is that what life with Lord Copeland would be? Her forever remaining more silent than was her nature when life with him got to be too mundane or too upsetting? Right now it felt like that would happen quite often. Would she be forced to repeatedly fake a headache and slip away to her room in solitude?

If it was, so be it.

She'd just seen Lady Helen. The woman was clearly miserable. Was life with the lieutenant so wholly wretched? Then again, what had Esther expected when she'd pushed the two together? It wasn't as though she'd imagined the two would miraculously fall in—

"Watch out!" Lord Copeland's call broke Esther's dark thoughts.

Lily Bay cried out, rearing back on her hind legs. Esther tightened her grip around the reins, yet they still slipped through her gloved hands. Esther fell back, sliding out of the saddle. For a moment, it felt as though she was motionless, frozen in air. Then the ground came up and collided with her body. The air left her lungs in a painful whoosh. Lord Copeland was calling out, but she couldn't make sense of his words. Everything felt muffled around her. The sounds, the sights—all of it was blurred and undefined.

She ached. Air entered her chest once more and she let out a groan. Lord Copeland knelt over her. Had he reined in Lily Bay? Was the mare calm once more? Being thrown was one thing, being trampled would be far worse.

"Lady Esther." Lord Copeland's head hovered above her own. "Are you all right?"

She most certainly was not, and if it had been Quintin kneeling next to her, she would have said as much. But this man, despite the fact that they'd spent much time together, was not someone she could be so frank with. "I am fine ... I believe."

He slipped an arm under her and helped her sit. Her spine felt quite stiff and she was certain she would be sore for days. Nonetheless, she could move her arms and legs.

"Nothing appears broken," she said.

"That's a relief."

The sound of a carriage rolling came from behind. "May we be of assistance?"

Drat. Lieutenant Fallow and Lady Helen were back. As much as she desperately wanted to avoid them, Esther did not feel she could ride Lily Bay back to the house.

Soon, she was settled, seated quite compactly beside Lady Helen. The woman refused to look even once at Esther.

It was just as well. Esther had nothing to say to her either.

It was a long and uncomfortable ride home.

CHAPTER 22

*E*sther stood before the front door, fingers twisting so hard around one another that her knuckles hurt. How long did it take for a butler to answer the door? Esther glanced about herself. She hadn't needed more than a spencer jacket today, it was so warm. Standing before Fallow's front door, it felt positively scorching. Esther ached to remove her bonnet and fan herself with it. A soft tearing sound brought her eyes around and down to her hands.

Drat. A seam along the fingers of her left glove had split. It seemed her fidgeting had finally done its worst. She clamped her jaw tight and shook her head, silently reprimanding herself. A grown woman should certainly be able to hold still while waiting for a butler. Perhaps she would never outgrow her need to move.

The door *finally* opened. The butler was younger than she'd expected, with no wrinkles and only a few stripes of gray in his hair. With hardly a word, he led her into the house, down a dark hallway, and into a small sitting room.

A thin woman, hair loose around her shoulders sat near a low-burning fire in the hearth. The butler left with even fewer words than he'd spoken when he had first opened the door.

Esther opened her mouth but paused. Taking another step

forward, she watched the woman closely. That wasn't Lady Helen, though she did look slightly familiar. Suppose Lieutenant Fallow had taken a mistress? Suppose this was her and he had decided to have her live side by side with his wife?

Esther shuddered at the thought. But surely not. Lieutenant Fallow wasn't *that* horrid a man ... right?

"Welcome," the woman said, standing. She was even thinner than Esther had originally assumed her to be. Gaunt, nearly. "I am sorry to say that my dear sister-in-law felt quite unequal to meeting with you this morning and is still abed."

Sister-in-law. Prickling panic rushed out of Esther in a single whoosh. Of course. Esther stepped forward, feeling quite foolish for her first assumption. "I do hope it isn't anything serious."

"No, I think it is rather too much society and too many late nights." The woman did have a nice smile, one Esther thought she'd seen before. There was something in her eyes Esther also thought she recognized. It looked like deep weariness, or even heartache. Still her smile did appear sincere. "I don't believe we've had the pleasure. I am Miss Rebecca Fallow."

"Lady Esther," Esther responded slowly, though her mind raced. Miss Rebecca. The woman Mother's friend had been concerned over, the one who'd been dancing with a blackguard at the beginning of the Season. The sister Lieutenant Fallow had desperately needed to return home to protect.

"Please, have a seat," Miss Rebecca continued, motioning toward the sofa across from her chair. "I've already rang for tea and cake."

"Thank you." This wouldn't prove to be the conversation Esther had expected this morning. She'd been fully ready to confess all to Lady Helen and beg her forgiveness. This conversation could be far better or far worse depending on what Miss Rebecca had to say about her brother's marriage.

"I understand you and Lady Helen were somewhat acquainted in India," Miss Rebecca said.

It was where everything had begun. Lieutenant Fallow's

seeking her out, pushing her into an impossible situation. Her turning on Lady Helen to save herself. But Esther was done running from the past. It was time she faced it. "Yes, we were out a bit in the same society. Does she speak of India much?"

"No." A bit of Miss Rebecca's smile faded. "Neither of them does."

A bit of awkward silence descended, most uncomfortably, between them. Esther knew fully well why neither of them spoke of India; it didn't hold pleasant memories for either Lieutenant Fallow or Lady Helen.

Blessedly, a couple of maids entered with a tea service and platter of finger cakes. Neither Esther nor Miss Rebecca said anything as the maids arranged things on the low table between them. Wordlessly, the maids slipped back out of the room, leaving the door nearly shut behind them.

Nothing broke the silence.

Miss Rebecca seemed nearly as uncomfortable as Esther felt. Esther became suddenly aware that her fingers were twisting about each other once more. Setting her jaw, Esther squeezed her hands together and silently, though also adamantly, reminded them to remain still.

"Tea?" Miss Rebecca said finally, scooting forward in her seat and picking up the teapot.

"Yes, thank you." Esther couldn't sit here for a quarter of an hour, speaking about the weather and other inane topics. She took the cup from Miss Rebecca and forced some words out. "Have you been enjoying England?" All right, so she would breach the more delicate subject of Lieutenant Fallow and Lady Helen in a moment. Esther felt like shaking her head at herself again; never had she had such a hard time filling a conversation.

"Oh yes, much more so now that my brother has returned."

There was something in her tone that was simply dripping with heartfelt gratitude. Lieutenant Fallow's need to return to England for his sister was quite well founded, it would seem.

"I'm glad to hear that." Esther took a quick breath and jumped in. "How is your new sister-in-law enjoying England?" She almost added "and married life," but that would have been too forward, especially coming from a near stranger.

Miss Rebecca's head tipped back and forth from side to side. "I am sure you already ascertained while with her in India that Lady Helen is a shy and quiet woman. I have learned that large crowds quite intimidate her."

"I saw the same thing in her in India." It was one of the aspects which had made it easy to push Lieutenant Fallows toward her. Guilt, sour and heavy, churned in Esther's stomach.

"Do you happen to know," Miss Rebecca said, placing her teacup back on the low table, "does Lady Helen perhaps enjoy musicales or the opera more than balls?"

"I'm sorry, I don't. We had very limited gatherings in India. Picnics and supper parties and the like, but no opera and only one musicale the entire time I was there."

Miss Rebecca stood suddenly, moved around the table, and sat herself directly beside Esther. "Since their return from India," her voice dropped quite low, probably to prevent any passing maid from overhearing, "I feel Lady Helen has been most unhappy. My brother is beside himself trying to cheer her up, but nothing seems to do the trick. Please excuse my boldness in speaking so directly."

Did Miss Rebecca not know then? Was it Esther's place to tell? Probably not, but, then again ... Oh, drat. Esther had to say something. She needed Miss Rebecca's help and it was now clear that Miss Rebecca needed Esther's. Secrets weren't going to get this problem solved.

"I'll excuse your boldness if you will excuse mine," Esther said. "Have neither of them told you the nature of their engagement and marriage?"

Miss Rebecca's eyes widened with uncertainty. "No, I can't say that they have."

Esther turned on the sofa and faced the woman more fully. She didn't hold any details back. She explained the whole of what had happened in India. Lieutenant Fallow's attentions toward herself, then his attempt to trap Esther into an engagement, Esther's desperate need to be free and her bringing up Lady Helen as an alternative, and finally society's shock at their quick engagement only a few months later. Miss Rebecca listened without interruption, her eyes only growing wider and her face more pale.

"Please, you must believe me, I have been quite distraught since then," Esther finished. "I know what I did was wrong, and I am most grievously sorry for it."

"I can't believe he did that," Miss Rebecca said, her voice weak. "He's always been so kind toward me." It seemed she couldn't reconcile the man Esther had described with the one she lived with.

Esther placed a hand atop the woman's. "He did tell me he needed to return to England to protect his sister. I believe he did it all with only you in mind."

Miss Rebecca blinked a few times, though her eyes continued to grow more red. "He did that for me?"

"I believe so."

Miss Rebecca leaned back against the sofa. "I had no idea. Poor Helen, no wonder she's been miserable. I just assumed they'd been happy in India and her melancholy had set on her since returning."

"I want you to know," Esther said, "that I am determined to set things to right. I am at fault here, and so the remedy must be mine as well."

"But what is to be done?"

"I'm not sure." Esther placed her own teacup back on the low table. It had grown cold during her recounting of India, though it didn't appeal to her anymore, regardless. She could not undo the marriage between Fallow and Helen, but was there possibly something else she could do to help the woman? "Do you think Lady Helen would appreciate having a friend here in London? She would not have to worry about sitting alone at balls or the like. Perhaps then they would be more bearable?" Her own father had announced a few nights before that he'd received an invitation from a friend for a short visit to the country. It had reminded Esther what a difference having a friend nearby could make. Well, his passing comment as well as the stark hole left by Quintin being gone.

"Perhaps." Miss Rebecca didn't sound certain in the least. "My brother rarely leaves her side during such events and he's always introducing her to others. He's told me more than once that he hopes she'll strike up a friendship with some woman or another."

Esther's brow pulled low. She'd always assumed that once Lieutenant Fallow had married and been allowed to return to England, a man like that would practically toss his wife aside and not bother with her again. But Miss Rebecca certainly had not painted their marriage in such a light. "What did you mean when you said that your brother is beside himself trying to cheer her up?"

"Oh, he's tried so many things. They've gone to nearly every supper party in Town. He's encouraged her to play at musicales, though she nearly fainted when he pressed. He's taken her out riding, even taking her out well before the fashionable hour so that the crowds will not overwhelm her."

That was why they were at Hyde Park the morning she and Lord Copeland had seen them.

"Nothing seems to make a bit of difference," Miss Rebecca continued. "I do think it has been rather trying on my brother."

Trying on Lieutenant Fallow? Well if anyone deserved it, he did. "He did bring such a thing upon himself, you recall." Esther regretted the snippish remark the moment it left her mouth. Miss Rebecca clearly thought quite highly of her brother.

"Perhaps he did. Rest assured I will be speaking to him on the subject."

There was no "perhaps" in what the lieutenant did. But Esther kept that remark to herself.

"Regardless," Miss Rebecca pressed, "does that necessitate they *both* be miserable for the rest of their lives?"

What else had the lieutenant expected when he pressed someone to marry him? Then again ... Miss Rebecca did have a point. "What your brother did was wrong, there's no denying that," Esther said. "But I see what you're saying as well. In full honesty, I had come this morning, hoping to help Lady Helen endure a life with an unpleasant husband. I feel her current situation is as much my fault as it is your brother's. But, very possibly, what Lady Helen needs is help in seeing more than her husband's one awful mistake." The statement felt right, the idea leaving a feeling of peace inside of Esther. Not until that moment did Esther realize how full of turmoil her life had become. To suddenly feel at peace again was like the calm after a thunderstorm. It was like a heavy stone had been lifted from her chest.

"Yes," Miss Rebecca said, her smile returning in full. "That's what we must do."

"Mind you," Esther said, not wanting Miss Rebecca to get ahead of herself. "Lady Helen and I were never close in India. There's a very good chance she will spurn my attempts to help her now." Especially after she learned the truth of Esther's role in her marriage.

"We must try, regardless," Miss Rebecca said. "My brother did everything for me. He came home and took me away from Father —" her voice choked suddenly, and she looked down. Esther had heard rumors of how heavy-handed Miss Rebecca's father could be. Miss Rebecca seemed to regain her composure all at once, sitting up straight again and facing Esther. "Don't ever worry that Lady Helen will have to face such a thing as my mother, and I did. My brother is quite a better man."

It seemed that Lieutenant Fallow was proving to be a better man all around—not just better than his own father but better than Esther had assumed him to be.

"You're right," Esther said. "They both deserve a second chance at a happy marriage."

CHAPTER 23

*T*he sheep doctor had finally arrived.

Quintin rode out with him posthaste to Martin Soames's land. They spent the entire hot day in the muck and fields. The doctor was clearly competent. He looked over many of the sheep, checked the stream they drank from and the grass they ate. Finally he declared that the sheep simply lacked nutrition. The land had had so many sheep roaming it for so many years, that it was struggling to grow the plants the sheep most needed. Essentially, there were too many sheep on too small a plot of land, and it had been that way for too long.

As the sun began to hang heavy in the sky, Quintin mounted his horse once more and began toward home.

"It shouldn't take long," Doctor Faust said in his deep voice. "Once they have a bit more room to roam and a bit more variety on which to graze, they'll be healthy and whole again. I know of a better supplier of hay, too. He's a bit more expensive, but the sheep will fare better in the winter."

So long as they didn't lose half the flock like they nearly did last winter, Quintin didn't mind the extra cost. "I cannot thank you enough."

The doctor only shrugged. "Only doing my job."

Still, it meant a lot to Quintin. In an effort to keep Cottonhold floating, he'd cut many corners, slimmed down as much of the cost as he could. Now he was beginning to see how, in some cases, he'd been hurting Cottonhold more than helping it. It was good to know where to spend more and where to not.

John had actually smiled the other day—first time that Quintin could remember the man ever doing so. With better times finally on the horizon, it seemed a fitting time for a first smile.

"I liked your idea to convert the farm to the East to more grazing land," Doctor Faust continued. "I think that will be a wise move."

"I'm glad you think so." It hadn't been producing much in the way of crops, so it wouldn't be a huge loss. One of the only benefits of having a failing estate.

They arrived at the house quickly and while stabling the horses, Quintin invited Doctor Faust to stay for dinner, an offer the man quickly accepted.

"Lord Dunn wasted no time in assuring me that Cottonhold's cook is one of the best in the land," Doctor Faust said with a chuckle.

Stepping from the stable, Quintin's stride came to an abrupt halt at seeing two men near the door.

"There you are," Dunn said. "I was beginning to worry that you wouldn't be back before supper. The gentleman I was telling you about—the one who's good at finding tenants—has arrived."

Quintin couldn't take his eyes off the newcomer.

Next to Dunn stood Lord Harrington, Esther's father.

THE NEXT WEEK WAS TENSE.

Quintin had known that Dunn was a good friend of Lord Harrington. Esther had told him as much. But he had never dreamed that when Dunn said he had a good friend who could help Quintin that he'd meant Lord Harrington. Or that Lord Harrington would come to Cottonhold. The man must have known he was coming to Quintin's estate.

That first evening together, Lord Harrington voiced more than a few jabs, first regarding Quintin's appearance after spending the day with his sheep farmer, and then about the sad state of his house. The next few days, it was all about how pitiful his tenants were performing and how little Quintin seemed to know about being a master.

This was precisely why Quintin hadn't asked for help to begin with. Then again, if this is what it took to become successful, he would weather it. He took Lord Harrington's terse comments in stride.

The evening before his guests were scheduled to return to London, Quintin sat back in a large chair, listening to Dunn and Lord Harrington chat easily. He'd developed a comfortable friendship with Dunn during the man's stay. Moreover, he even felt that he was no longer in Lord Harrington's black book, though he still wasn't exactly congenial.

"Well," Dunn said rocking forward and taking hold of his cane. "I think it best I turn in. If we're leaving at first light, I need to get to bed."

"I can't thank you enough for coming to Cottonhold," Quintin said, remaining in his seat.

"Think nothing of it. I struggled for far longer than you have before I figured out how to master an estate." He slowly made his way toward the door, his age evident in each step. "Though I must admit, I am quite anxious to see my Sarah again." Standing in the doorway, he turned back toward the room. "You coming, Harrington?"

"No," Harrington said, his gaze on the fire. "I think I shall sit for a bit longer."

Quintin bid Dunn a good night, but his eyes returned to his other guest the moment the older man had left the room. Lord Harrington had been somewhat quiet during their workday, though he'd spoken easily enough with Dunn afterward. Come to think of it, he hadn't made a single derogatory remark toward Quintin all day. Perhaps he'd been saving them up for just such a moment as this.

Or perhaps the man simply was tired and needed some time to himself. Quintin could certainly relate to that.

"I shall retire as well," Quintin said, standing, "and give you some quiet."

"Sit," Harrington ordered. The man sighed. "Please," he amended.

Quintin wasn't sure what the man had on his mind, but he felt fairly sure it wasn't going to bring a pleasant conversation. Still, he sat back in his chair once more.

"Quintin," Harrington started, using his Christian name for the first time since arriving, "I feel I ought to apologize for that day in White's."

Quintin didn't have to ask what he was referring to. Having the father of the woman you loved declare in no uncertain terms that you were never to see her again was not something a man forgot quickly.

"I judged you too hastily. I see that now." The words almost seemed as though he had to pull them out unwillingly. "I've watched you this past week. You may not say much, but you're a hard worker and you care about your tenants."

"Thank you, sir." Quintin felt obligated to say it, though he still wasn't confident in the direction of their conversation.

"I have no doubt that Cottonhold will grow to be one of the most profitable and highly esteemed estates in the county. You've shown me that you don't need a dowry or anything else. You know how to push on in the hard times and you aren't afraid to get your hands dirty."

This was high praise indeed. Quintin wasn't at all sure how to respond.

"I guess, what I'm trying to say is . . ." Lord Harrington leaned forward, resting his forearms against his knees. "I'm sorry things didn't work out between you and Esther. I would have been proud to call you my son."

Quintin felt his mouth go a bit slack.

Had Lord Harrington truly said what he *thought* the man had just said?

Pushing off his knees, Lord Harrington stood. "I best be turning in myself. Good night, Quintin." He strode toward the door purposefully, probably anxious to end this unexpected and almost awkward conversation as quickly as possible.

Quintin just sat.

Slowly, he leaned further back into the chair and slumped. Lord Harrington would have been proud to have called him son. Quintin peered down into the cup in his hand. He certainly hadn't seen that one coming. Not that it mattered now. Not really.

Quintin downed the contents in his cup and stood quickly before thoughts of Esther and what would never be took over him. He moved out of the room and toward his bedchamber. Lord Harrington's words followed him the entire way.

It was a win, no doubt about it. But without Esther, every win was hollow.

CHAPTER 24

*F*or two weeks now, Esther had been trying to speak with Lady Helen. Apparently, she was not as oblivious to Esther's role in her forced marriage as she'd originally assumed. Either that, or Esther was enough of a reminder of India that seeing her alone was proving too much for Lady Helen to bear.

Either way, Esther was growing more and more determined that they speak. It was perhaps anticlimactic. Any story she and Quintin had read ended with the hero and heroine braving dragons or jungles to reach one another. Usually there was a bit of sword fighting, too. Sitting down, as two adult women, and having an honest conversation seemed quite dull in comparison.

At the same time, it seemed far more frightening.

Esther would have gladly rather taken a sword in hand and faced a fire breathing dragon than sit across from Lady Helen and confess what she'd done.

Nonetheless, Miss Rebecca—whom Esther had been in close contact with—was certain she could get Lady Helen out of the house and to the Wheatons' supper party tomorrow. The Wheatons were not known for their large or lavish gatherings. No doubt, this one tomorrow would prove quite demure in comparison to most of

London's offerings, which was why Miss Rebecca could get Lady Helen to commit to attending at all.

Now, it was Esther's turn. Convincing Mother to attend a small, quiet supper party and pass up the many larger gatherings they'd been invited to would prove every bit as hard as Miss Rebecca convincing Lady Helen to leave her solitude. Father, recently returned from his trip to the country, would go wherever Mother wanted. Truth was, he'd been a bit more wistful since his return. Almost sad. He'd even kissed Esther on the forehead every morning since he'd come back. It was a bit strange, but she would piece out that puzzle another time.

"Good morning, Mother," Esther said, moving through the breakfast room doors.

"There you are, darling," Mother said, hardly looking up from that morning's stack of letters. "I trust you slept well?"

"Yes, thank you." Esther picked up a plate and filled it with a bit of ham and some potatoes. "I understand we received an invitation from the Wheatons."

Mother still did not look up, even as Esther sat across from her. "I believe we did. But we'll be busy attending Almack's, tomorrow. We've not been in two weeks."

Her mother made "two weeks" sound like nearly two years. "Do you not think the Wheatons' gathering would be quite diverting as well?"

"As diverting as Almacks? Seriously, Esther dear, sometimes I worry for you."

Esther let out a small breath of frustration. This was just how mother had acted in India. She'd dismissed Esther's fears and pushed her to go where there was society and friends, regardless.

"I truly would prefer to go to the Wheatons'." Esther couldn't back down as she had in India. Then, she'd caved when Mother refused to listen to her. Esther had hinted at wanting to avoid a certain man, and Mother had shaken her head and said not to fret so. Esther had hedged around the idea of going somewhere else instead, or possibly even being left home while Mother and Father went out. But none of it had worked.

Esther wasn't going to do that again. She wasn't going to hint or hedge. She would come right out and say what she wanted and why. No more keeping uncomfortable secrets tucked away.

"Mother," Esther said, her voice firm. For the first time that morning, Mother looked up at her. "Do you remember Lady Helen? We met her in India."

"You mean that quiet thing who married Lieutenant Fallow?"

Esther nodded. "She has returned to London and will be at the Wheatons' tomorrow, I understand."

"So? You two were never close. I don't see why her appearance should alter our plans."

"You know how very reserved she is. I feel she would appreciate having a friend nearby."

"She very well might," Mother said, returning her gaze to the letters before her. "But that still doesn't mean *you* should go. You are nothing to her, I am sure."

Mother was right on that account. Esther and Lady Helen had never been more than passing acquaintances. "That may be true, but I am more to her than anyone else at the Wheatons' will be. Besides, we are more to one another than passing acquaintances now." Before her courage would dissolve, Esther told her mother what happened in India. She didn't go into as many details as she had with Quintin or Miss Rebecca. For some strange reason, this retelling was hardest of all.

Mother disagreed many times, interrupting and even trying to quit the breakfast room altogether at one point. Still, Esther pressed on and got the whole of it out.

"I spoke with Lieutenant Fallow's sister the other day. She and I are in agreement. He and Lady Helen may be happy together if only she will give him another chance. That is why I want to go to the Wheatons'. I wish to see her and speak with her."

"You plan to tell her all that you've told me?" Mother's tone was softer than normal.

"Yes. Tell her and then see if I can't help her."

"She will hate you, you realize. She very well may feed you to the gossipmongers."

It would be no less than she deserved. "Either way, this is something I feel I must do."

Mother shook her head. "You are young, and doubtless your heart is in the right place. But—"

"Mother," Esther said, standing. "I am going to the Wheatons' tomorrow and I will speak with Lady Helen. It would be far less a scandal if I did not arrive alone."

Mother's face actually grew slightly pale at that. It wasn't that Esther wanted to hurt her mother. But Esther absolutely *had* to see and speak with Lady Helen.

"Very well, then." Mother regained her composure. "I will write to the Wheatons this morning and let them know we will be attending."

"Thank you, Mother."

Esther had finally gotten her mother to listen; it was slightly thrilling. It certainly made her feel braver and stronger than she had since leaving India.

At the same time, it meant she would most certainly be meeting with Lady Helen tomorrow. For that conversation, Esther would need all the bravery and strength she could find.

CHAPTER 25

*E*sther stood near a far wall, waiting for the rest of the ladies to enter the drawing room.

Lady Helen was here, as well as her husband and Miss Rebecca. Esther had seen them the moment they'd arrived, only ten minutes after herself and her parents. Esther had spoken with them for a bit. Miss Rebecca had been kind and even a bit talkative. Lieutenant Fallow had been polite, but Esther had sensed the tension between him and his wife. The conversation had ended quickly. The other before-supper conversations Esther had engaged in had not been able to ease her apprehension the least bit. Supper itself had felt tedious and drawn out.

Finally, the women had withdrawn and left the men to their port. Now would be Esther's best opportunity to speak with Lady Helen. Miss Rebecca entered the drawing room, Lady Helen beside her. It seemed like Miss Rebecca was trying to convince Lady Helen to walk deeper into the room, and closer to Esther. But Lady Helen shook her head and sat in a corner, far from everyone else.

Miss Rebecca glanced over at Esther, uncertainty and concern evident in her expression. Well, at least Lady Helen had finally

found one person she could say no to. It was just rather unfortunate
that it was here and now.

Esther smoothed her skirt. If Lady Helen wouldn't come to her,
she would go to Lady Helen. Moving across the room, Esther didn't
stop to greet any of the other ladies. She moved directly up to Lady
Helen, not giving her a chance to avoid the conversation.

"Hello again," Esther began. "It is good to see you."

Lady Helen glanced her way, but only nodded silently.

"I must say, this room is proving crowded, even with the men
still absent. Would you do the pleasure of taking a turn with me
about the garden?" There they would be able to speak in private.

"I believe I would rather sit," Lady Helen said, her voice so low
Esther almost didn't hear it.

Esther didn't want to force her into anything; she'd done
enough of that already. Still, the conversation needed to happen.
"All right, if you wish to stay," Esther said, taking hold of a nearby
chair and pulling it closer, "I will sit with you."

Lady Helen didn't respond at all to that, though she pointedly
kept her gaze off Esther.

Sitting quite close to Lady Helen, Esther didn't need her voice to
be anything louder than a whisper to be heard. "I understand that
you have been unhappy since returning to England." Perhaps a
gentle woman like Lady Helen would have been better handled
with more subtlety, but Esther wasn't good at such things.

"England is all right," Lady Helen said.

"But you are not."

Lady Helen blinked rapidly. "It's only been so long since I've
been home, I'd forgotten how loud it is. I cannot say I enjoy having
so many people about."

Esther felt a moment of elation. That was more than she'd ever
heard Lady Helen say at one time. This might just work after all.
"And while you're at home? With only the lieutenant and his sister
about, surely the house is quiet enough for your liking?"

Lady Helen's posture slumped. Esther hated bringing up something she knew would be unpleasant, especially when they were

just on the verge of starting a real conversation where more than just Esther did the talking. But this had to happen.

"The house is quite comfortable," Lady Helen said, her voice catching slightly.

Oh dear, the woman looked quite near falling apart. "Perhaps you would like that turn about the garden now?"

"Yes," she stated quickly, rising from her seat faster than Esther had expected. "Yes, I feel it is getting quite stuffy in here."

They moved together past the various clusters of women, all chatting and laughing, through the far doors and out into the evening. The Wheatons had a small, though well-tended, garden. The moment they were outside, Lady Helen lengthened her stride and walked in front of Esther. She reached a row of roses and bent to smell them.

Esther watched her, suddenly unsure how to begin. She needed to tell Lady Helen everything. She was determined she would.

"I know," Lady Helen said, standing once more. "I know that you encouraged Lieutenant Fallow and redirected his addresses toward me."

"Lady Helen, I am so sorry." The words burst from Esther, even as she hurried forward to stand directly beside the woman. "I was scared. I panicked."

"It's all right." Lady Helen's voice grew lifeless. "It was nothing less than what any other woman would have done. It was only me you hurt, after all." Lady Helen turned away from Esther and continued to move along the row of roses, stopping to smell another one.

"Only you?" Esther repeated. Did the woman truly think so poorly of herself? "No. What I did was wrong. I knew it even then." If only Lady Helen would stop walking away and just hear her out. "I do not mean to excuse myself, only to explain. I was frightened—"

"Like a horse seeing a snake."

Esther paused, her mind jumping back to Lily Bay, throwing her at Hyde Park. "Yes," she said. "Very much like that."

"Then you see, I already understand," Lady Helen said, facing her at last. "I know how it feels to do—to become—something you are not proud of because you are scared."

How was it that Lady Helen, quiet and reserved, understood so much better than Esther had herself?

"You have every right to hate me," Esther said.

"I did," Lady Helen replied. "But only for a time. After a while, I grew to see what I didn't want to see at first."

"That I'm a horse?" Esther said, hoping to lighten the heavy air between them.

Lady Helen's lips twitched. "Something like that."

Esther hesitated to say what needed to be asked next. "And what of the lieutenant?"

The slight humor of before faded immediately. "He is my husband. What else is there to be said on the subject?"

"You forgave me. Have you forgiven him?" Esther couldn't believe she was speaking up on Lieutenant Fallow's behalf. A month ago she would have gladly had the man shipped to South America to fend for himself among the wilds there if the opportunity had arisen. But in wanting to make things right, she'd changed. Speaking with Miss Rebecca had shed a new light on things. Actively seeking out Lady Helen's forgiveness had both strengthened and softened her.

"I think I will return inside," Lady Helen said, making as though to move past.

"Please." Esther stopped her with a gentle hand on her arm. "Hear me out."

Lady Helen, much to Esther's surprise, did stop and face her, appearing quite willing to listen.

"I think there's something to be said for him as well. I am sure you are more aware than I of Mr. Fallow's nature. Miss Rebecca needed the lieutenant to save her; for him to return home he needed a wife."

Lady Helen didn't say anything.

"You know what it's like to be scared. Perhaps that's how he was feeling, too."

"He isn't a horse." Her tone turned harsh for the first time. "Or even a woman. He is a *man* and that means he has more options, more opportunities, than you or I could ever hope to have."

"Yes, but that doesn't mean he wasn't backed against a wall. Miss Rebecca was hurting, and it was only him who could save her. The army wasn't going to let him return to England for no reason, not even to visit."

"I'm sure he could have found another way." She blinked again and looked down. Like an old, weathered wall, Lady Helen seemed to be crumbling right before Esther's eyes. "He and my father drew up the papers, forcing me into this marriage for personal gain and sport."

"Your father?"

Lady Helen's hand covered her mouth and her shoulders shuddered. She truly seemed on the cusp of crying. "Fallow didn't corner me the same way he cornered you. There was no moonlight stroll in the hopes I'd become blind to his true intention. He met with my father. I knew they were meeting but had no reason to think twice about it. Then, at supper that night, father announced I was engaged to the man. There was no chance to face him. No chance to defend myself. It was done and the papers signed before I was even aware."

Her own father had done this to her? Esther's own father may not be fully engaged in her life. He often preferred a quiet room to anything else. But she never once had feared he would force her into a marriage she did not want. The new facts struggled against the images of India that she'd held tight to for so very long.

Esther thought Fallow had led Lady Helen into a compromising situation, just as he'd wanted to do to her. Only now, thinking back over the gossip which had run wild after the engagement was made known, Esther saw the obvious. If Fallow and Lady Helen had been *found* in a compromising situation together, *someone* would have had to do the finding. No one had ever claimed to have seen them within arm's length of each other. All this time, Esther had seen the blame as wholly her own and Fallow's. But, truthfully, if Lady Helen's father had only done the decent thing, the marriage would not have taken place. Esther felt a modicum of relief, and also a bit foolish to have thought, this entire time, that she alone had ruined Lady Helen's life.

Lady Helen drew in a deep breath, most likely trying to calm herself. "Claiming that he was acting to protect Rebecca only occurred to Fallow later."

"It wasn't like that," Esther said. "He told me, well before he ever set any designs on you, that he was desperate to return to England to save his sister."

Lady Helen didn't respond, but Esther got the impression she was still listening.

"I truly believe he never intended to hurt you. He was simply too crazed at the thought of his father being left unchecked around his sister to think of anything, or anyone else."

Lady Helen let out a shuddering breath. "He does dote on her quite excessively." There was no bitterness in the words, no jealousy, only acknowledgment.

"I spoke with Miss Rebecca the other day. She said her brother is quite beside himself wanting to make you happy but is unsure how to do it."

Lady Helen finally looked up, her brow creased. "That cannot be. He is embarrassed by me, I am sure."

"Why do you think that?"

"He is continually taking me out into society, pushing me to do or be something. I'm not even sure what. Only, it seems I never measure up."

"I think he's hoping you will enjoy some activity or another enough to be happy."

She shook her head, slowly at first, but it quickly grew more rapid. "No. No, I cannot believe so." Lady Helen pushed past Esther.

"Is there nothing you truly like?" Esther called after her. She felt certain the lieutenant only needed a hint, a direction to take. Miss Rebecca was certain if he only knew what his wife liked she'd have it in spades. Esther couldn't fix the fact that they were married, nor could she change either of their natures so that they were a better fit. But she could help nudge them toward one another. She could speak up and show the courage she'd forgotten she had inside.

Lady Helen slowed as she reached the back door. They hadn't gone far from the house and so Lady Helen was still only a pace or two away.

"Flowers," she said slowly.

"Excuse me?" Esther asked, unsure what Lady Helen was saying.

Lady Helen angled her chin toward Esther but didn't turn fully around. "I like flowers." Her voice grew yet more soft. "And dresses." She hurried back inside the house, though Esther thought she saw a small blush creep up her cheeks at admitting such things.

Esther stood for a moment. It may not have been much—certainly no grandstand against an enemy army—but it had been heart-wrenching. And perhaps, not entirely fruitless. Esther followed Lady Helen's course and reentered the house. The men were in the drawing room now, not only the ladies. Esther spotted Lady Helen easily enough, making her way back toward the corner.

Lieutenant Fallow saw his wife as well and followed her. Esther couldn't hear what they were saying, but he did smile at her and seemed to try to be encouraging her to speak with others. Esther felt bad for both of them. Lieutenant Fallow only wanted his wife to be happy. Now that his sister was safe, there was every chance that he realized what a hard thing he'd done to Lady Helen and felt as guilty as Esther had all these months.

Lady Helen only wanted to be loved and accepted as she was. As such, she was misreading his endeavors of diverting her with all the pleasures of Town as a show that he didn't care for her quiet nature.

As they spoke, Lady Helen looked up at her husband. Esther

didn't know her well enough to fully understand what the look in her eye meant. But if she had to guess, it certainly looked as though Lady Helen was considering her husband in a new light.

"Well?" Miss Rebecca stepped up beside Esther. "How did it go?"

"She didn't realize that you were the lieutenant's main reason for pressing her into a marriage. She thought he'd done it for sport."

"Oh, gracious."

"And I didn't realize that her own father is as much to blame as your brother or myself."

"I learned as much only yesterday," Miss Rebecca said, "when I confronted my brother about this whole thing."

That couldn't have been pleasant.

"He told me," Miss Rebecca turned and faced Esther fully, "that it was because of the fear he saw in you the night he tried to force your hand that he chose to take a different path with Lady Helen. After leaving you that night, he swore to himself that he would never do that again. So he approached Lady Helen's father and offered for her hand. The man was apparently far too pleased to get rid of her and pushed him into signing the papers posthaste." Miss Rebecca shook her head in blatant bitterness against Lady Helen's father. "Until yesterday I hadn't even considered the part her own family might have played."

Nor had Esther, though it seemed an egregious error on her part now. And apparently, her short time with Fallow had not only left her changed, but him as well. She was glad for it. "Lady Helen did admit that she doesn't care to be pushed out into society so much. She thinks your brother wants her to be someone she's not."

"That's not it at all. Only, every other woman my brother knows *loves* society."

"Perhaps you might explain to him?"

Miss Rebecca nodded.

"Also." Esther leaned in a bit closer to her new friend. "She admitted to liking flowers and new dresses."

A small smile slipped over Miss Rebecca's lips. "I think that's just the thing my brother needs to know." The lieutenant looked over his shoulder just then and beckoned to Miss Rebecca.

"Looks like you are leaving," Esther said.

"Thank you for speaking with her." Miss Rebecca gave Esther a quick hug. "Don't worry. I have a feeling they'll be all right now."

"I most certainly hope so." There wasn't anything more Esther could do now. It would be up to the lieutenant to do what he would with the information Miss Rebecca gave him. It would be up to Lady Helen to choose how to respond. Whatever happened, Esther had done what she could.

Miss Rebecca pulled back slightly. "And what of you, my friend? Will you be all right now as well?"

The question surprised Esther. She blinked and for a moment didn't know how to respond.

"We haven't been friends for long," Miss Rebecca continued. "But I have to admit that even I am aware there are two gentlemen vying for your hand."

Esther felt her throat thicken. She blinked again, though this time it wasn't in surprise, but to quell the sudden feeling of tears.

"Esther, dear," Miss Rebecca spoke softly. "No matter what happens between my brother and his wife, remember you will not make their situation any better for making your own miserable. Misery only breeds more misery. Love breeds love.

The heartache Esther had been most determined not to feel broke through, flooding over her and leaving her gasping for air.

"If you do still harbor any feeling of needing to make things right," Miss Rebecca continued, "then do it by pouring more love into the world, not less." With a smile, Miss Rebecca stepped away and moved toward her family.

Esther stood, silently watching, as the three Fallows left. She wasn't even sure what to think or feel. She hurt—she *ached* to be near Quintin again. Oh, how she'd missed him. Though she'd tried not to, ever since he'd left not a day had gone by where she hadn't wondered about him. Worried about his estate and how he was fairing. Pined for the sound of his voice, the ease of their conversations. Yearned for his arms around her, his lips against her own once again.

She'd told him that India had changed her and it had. But now, this Season had changed her as well. Seeing Joan and Will come to know one another, speaking with Quintin from opposite sides of the curtain at the opera, dancing at balls with Lord Copeland. All of it had changed her. Had healed her.

Now, all those wants and desires collided inside her. She loved Quintin, had always loved him, and she was done denying it. Moreover, she not only loved him, but now she loved herself enough to put aside the past and make a future.

It was time she do something about it, too.

But it would have to be something meaningful, something personal. Something that could only come from her, and something she would only do for Quintin.

Her smile grew, even as a rush of nervous excitement coursed through her.

She knew just the thing.

CHAPTER 26

"Quintin?" Venetia poked her head in.

He waved her fully inside, setting his pen down. "Come, have a seat." He motioned to the chair John had recently vacated.

"More good news?" she asked, sitting across from him.

"It looks like Cottonhold is going to be safe for another year."

"Only for a year?"

Quintin shrugged, trying not to let his smile get too big. "Honestly, I think it's going to become one of the biggest estates in the whole county someday."

"I never doubted it for a minute."

He chuckled softly. "I did. But not now." For the first time, he noticed a brown paper package in her lap. "Did Penelope send you something?"

Venetia's smile grew, so much that her eyes lit up like tiny candles. "Actually, it's from Esther." She stood, placing the package atop his desk. "And it isn't for me."

Quintin's heart flipped quite painfully at the name. Neither he nor Venetia had said *her* name since retiring to the country. Quintin had done his utmost to not even think of her. Yet, hearing only her name was enough to tear down all he'd built up against the memo-ries. Longing, desire, and all the other emotions he desperately didn't want to feel flooded into him.

He was trying to forget her. Trying to move on.

Trying, but failing.

"Women of breeding do not send gentlemen packages," Quintin said. Anything to stop the hope rising in his chest.

"Oh she didn't, not exactly. It was addressed to me," Venetia explained. "But she sent a note with it as well, asking if I would please see that you got this"—she tapped the package—"since, as you put it, a woman of breeding would never send a gentleman something." Happy as a lark, and not at all inclined to hide it, Venetia stood and nearly pranced to the door. "You know," she said, turning around once more. "You used nearly the exact same words she did in her letter. You two really are quite a match."

But they weren't a match. He couldn't let his hope get back up. He couldn't . . .

His eyes landed on the package before him, and he heard the door close behind Venetia.

Hope—cursed, painful, unwanted hope—burned triumphant over the other emotions vying for a place inside of him. Quintin reached out and snatched at the package. He quickly tore away the brown paper and twine.

It was a small book, the kind ladies often bought for sketches or the like. Quintin held perfectly still. She'd sent him a book. Simple though it was, it brought with it the remembrance of hours they'd spent together, him reading aloud to her, afternoons romping through the woods between their families' estates, pretending to battle enemy armies or giant venomous snakes.

He should open it.

But what was inside?

Excuses why they couldn't be together? A further explanation of how she'd changed since India and that he wasn't what she wanted anymore?

He opened the cover.

There was no title page. No name to whatever he held in his hands. Esther's girl-ish voice, from so many years ago, came to mind. "I don't care about the title, Quintin. Just get to the story."

He nearly smiled.

Still, trepidation wouldn't let him fully relax. He turned the blank, front page. Behind it, was a simple drawing. It was Esther's work; he knew it by sight.

She was painting again.

A warm comfort washed over him and Quintin momentarily shut his eyes. Though she would never agree to be his, he had still desperately hoped she would heal someday. Now he knew for certain she was making progress. She *was* healing. She was once more allowing happiness and love to grow within her.

Opening his eyes once more, Quintin ran a hand down the image. Though it was simple, it was the most beautiful watercolor he'd ever seen. Beautiful because it was so very like Esther.

It was of two children. A little boy and a little girl. The girl was his favorite; she was drawn with unruly hair and a large smile. The boy looked far cleaner than he ever remembered being as a child. Nonetheless, he knew it was him and her. No words graced the bottom of the page, though there was ample room left for them to be added.

He turned to the next page. It was them crossing a fallen log over a brook. The next was them lying on their stomachs, reading a book together. She'd captured the Ramport nursery perfectly. Then again, how could she not remember it as vividly as he? She'd spent nearly as many hours there as he himself had.

The next page: climbing a tree.

The next: her pushing him into the river.

Then the two of them together under the willow tree.

Quintin's breath caught. She'd captured the very moment he'd kissed her on the cheek. Of all the times they'd spent together, that was the one that he'd always wondered about. Did she think back on that moment as he did? He'd brought it up that one night, just outside the barn. She had not said if she could recall the memory or not; yet here the moment stood, drawn in soft watercolors against the page. She remembered. After all they'd been through, she remembered it as clearly as he did.

The next few pages covered much time. There was Esther waving goodbye to him as he left for University. He hadn't known she'd cried. There was Quintin studying over a book as she stood at the rail of a ship. He turned the page. They stood, backs toward one another, facing opposite sides of the page. She looked unsure, while a green background contrasted against the red rug beneath her feet. Esther had said there was a lot of red in India. He, on the other hand, stood with head hanging low. And ... was that a dead sheep at his feet?

Quintin barked out a short laugh. Well, she certainly had grasped the essence of his life without her. Life without Esther was like a dead sheep at one's feet, and in Quintin's case, literal dead sheep.

He turned the page. It was them at a ball. She was dancing with a man whose back was toward the viewer so that his face wasn't visible, but Esther was looking at Quintin. On the next page, he sat behind her at the musicale. Then the two of them were among a wall of ribbons, more focused on each other than the wares about them. On the next page, they rode together through Hyde Park, sharing a smile. Then they were at the Monstattens' home, Quintin beside a piano and Esther on the other side of the room. No other people were drawn in that picture, but neither of them were smiling. Quintin's chest constricted. Not all of their time together in London had been pleasant.

He turned the page. What could only be morning light spread across the image. They were standing close to one another, neither smiling nor scowling. Then, another page turn, and they were apart once more. Esther was on a horse, the other characters around her too blurry to make out. Quintin was hunched over a desk again. At least there were no dead sheep in the image.

Esther stood in a garden, talking to another woman, one Quintin didn't recognize. Whatever these last few pages were speaking of, they were of the time *after* Quintin had left London. His fingers hovered above the book. Did he really want to know what came next? Suppose it was an image of her on Lord Copeland's arm? Suppose it was an image of them, old and gray, and still apart?

But surely she wouldn't go through all this trouble just to tell him what he already knew—that she wasn't willing to accept him? This must have taken her days to complete. She wouldn't do all this just to hurt him.

Steeling himself, Quintin turned the page.

It was an image of Ester, sitting at a table, pages spread out before her, drawing. This was her making the book he held. She'd even replicated some of the earlier images onto the pages spread before herself in this picture.

The next image included them both. He breathed out a little relief, and then studied the image more. It was them, grown now, under the willow tree once more. Quintin's heart sped up. They stood facing one another, something between them. He looked closer. It was a book. The very book he held in his hands right now, if he wasn't mistaken.

Between him and Esther, they both held one end of the book. It was unclear if, in the image, Esther was handing it to him, or Quintin was handing it to her. They were looking at each other. Though neither had broad grins, they didn't wear the uneasy expressions so many earlier pictures had shown. If he had to describe the expression on both his and Esther's faces, he'd say they were hopeful.

There was only one image left.

Quintin turned the page.

The last paper was empty. No image, no message, no anything.

What did that mean?

The moment he wondered, he knew.

It meant their next step hadn't happened yet. It meant Esther was waiting to find out. She was *willing* to find out. He turned back to the second to last page, the one of the two of them beneath the willow tree.

He stood abruptly. His chair clattered to the side. Leaving it to lay as it was, Quintin sprinted to the door and threw it open.

"Venetia," he called. "Venetia."

She came hurrying out of the drawing room. "What is it?" She looked genuinely alarmed.

"We're returning to Ramport Manor immediately. How soon can you be packed?"

"What? Well, I don't—"

"We'll leave in an hour."

"Quintin, I can't possibly be ready by then."

"Bring only enough for the trip then and we'll have your maid come with the rest tomorrow."

"I suppose that would work."

"Good." He turned to reenter his book room, but then paused and turned back to Venetia. "Thanks for being with me these past few months."

"Of course," she said, still looking a bit unsteady.

"Now, you best hurry. I'm serious about leaving within the hour."

Venetia nodded and moved down the hall. Quintin leaned against the door frame and opened the book once more, flipping again to the second to last page.

He would claim that Venetia had grown tired of keeping house for him at last and he was simply returning her home to Ramport Manor. But while he was there, he'd be certain to visit the willow tree. His eyes moved down to the blank space along the bottom of the page.

Before he started packing, there was one other thing he needed to do.

CHAPTER 27

*E*sther stood beneath the long, arching bows of the willow tree. A soft summer breeze sent the branches swaying around her. Would today be the day he finally came? It hadn't been easy convincing Mother to retire to the country early. Esther would do it every year for decades if that's what it took to convince Quintin she loved him and she was ready to be his wife. Surprisingly, when Esther had petitioned Father for his thoughts, he had surprised them all and wholeheartedly agreed with her.

After speaking with Miss Rebecca and Lady Helen at the Wheatons' party, Esther had begun work on the book that very night. The next morning Lord Copeland had come to call. It had been a short conversation, but after she explained that she was truly in love with another, he'd offered her a deep bow and a sincere wish for her every happiness. He hadn't appeared overly distraught, only as civil and straightforward and boring as ever. Esther was glad; she had no intentions of hurting more hearts ever again. After she'd explained to her mother that Lord Copeland would not be calling on her again, she and Father were able to convince Mother that they should leave Town.

The only person she couldn't convince to come back to the

country was Joan. The young woman's eyes had veritably sparkled when she'd told Esther that Will had asked for her hand in marriage. Esther smiled at the memory. Joan was staying with a friend until the ceremony. Perhaps, if Mother's mood improved between now and then, she would allow Esther to attend the wedding. She still hadn't found a new abigail, but that had done nothing to dampen her own joy at Joan's happiness.

The wind picked up again, and leaves rustled all around her. Esther closed her eyes, listening to the sound that brought back so many childhood memories. She'd sent the book to Quintin the morning they'd left for home. After arriving, she'd began coming here every day. There was no way to know exactly when Quintin had received her gift, or how he felt about it, or how soon he would come.

Oh, she prayed he'd come.

If only he'd give her one more chance, she'd show him that she *did* love him, every bit as much as he loved her. She wanted him to hold her. Wanted to rest her head against his chest. To press her lips against his and know that his heart still beat for her.

"Hello, Esther."

Her eyes shot open. She hadn't heard him approach. Yet, there her Quintin stood. He was dressed well. Not as fine as while in London, but still he looked so very handsome. His eyes were hesitant, though she could see hope in them as well.

"Hello, Quintin."

They'd greeted each other so many times over the years, yet this time it felt strange. They'd been through too much this year for things to ever be the same. Then again, Esther didn't want them to be the same. She loved her childhood friend, but now she wanted something more.

Hanging at Quintin's side, clasped tightly in a gloved hand, was the little book she'd made.

"You got it," she said, motioning toward it. "I hope Venetia didn't mind me using her as a courier."

"If she did, she's far too put out with me for rushing her from Cottonhold to dwell on it."

She took a step closer to him. "I was hoping you'd come." Now that he was here, she was feeling at a loss as to what to say or do. Where had that time gone when every moment together was all ease and joy? Clearly, they'd gone and grown up.

He stepped closer as well, until they stood directly in front of one another. He held the book out. "I added to it."

"Did you?" It was all she could think to say.

She reached for the book. The moment her hands touched it, she remembered the last image she'd drawn, the two of them together beneath the willow tree, the book between them.

"I hope it's all right," Quintin said.

Hoped what was all right?

"What I did to the story," he quickly added.

She opened the cover. A title now graced the front page. *A Farewell Kiss*. The second word made her heart skip a beat; so did the third, but for wholly different reasons. She didn't know at all what to make of such a title.

"Read it," he whispered.

Esther nodded and turned the first page. Quintin's handwriting, sure and clear, paired perfectly with her image.

"Once upon a time," she read aloud, "there was a little girl and a little boy."

"Though the boy was always far dirtier than the pictures make him out to be," Quintin added softly.

She pursed her lips to keep from smiling like a fool and instead tried to scowl at him. "I thought you wanted me to read it."

He held up his hands in submission.

Esther turned the page to the image of them crossing a log above a small brook. "They had many adventures together for they both loved life too much to worry much about anything else."

She turned to the image of them reading together on their stomachs. "But above all, they loved stories. Princesses and knights.

Dragons and evil sorcerers. They devoured every book they could get their hands on."

A turn brought her to the picture of them in a tree. "When they couldn't be reading, they brought the stories to life in their own games. Trees became castles and squirrels their trusty surfs. Except when the squirrels darted to nearby trees. Then they were branded traitors and justifiably dismissed."

Esther laughed softly; she'd forgotten about the traitorous squirrels. The next page was of her pushing him into the river. "Sometimes, their parents thought they took their stories a touch too far." Her gaze jumped up to meet his. "Took it too far? You were teasing me. You said I was too weak to be a suitable general."

Quintin smiled. "Is that what happened? I couldn't quite remember."

"Oh, don't even try to pretend you've forgotten." She took a step forward, closing the space between them and placing a finger near his face. "You said *you* should be King *and* General. That I as a girl couldn't possibly . . ." She suddenly became fully aware of just how closely they stood. The book's pages were pressed against her stomach, no more space between them than that.

Quintin reached up and took hold of her accusatory finger and held it between his own. Heat, comfortable yet heady, rushed through her at the touch.

"Don't worry," he said, his voice far steadier than she felt. "You proved me quite wrong. I've never doubted your strength since."

Esther couldn't seem to pull her gaze away from him. His blue eyes, so very familiar, now tugged at her in a way that she'd only dreamed of before. Had it been there all along? Had she truly been so very blinded by her own shame to have missed it?

"You should keep reading," he said softly, though his gaze jumped down to her lips before coming back up again.

Esther nodded and took a small step back, just enough that she could see the book once more.

A turn of the page brought her to the image of them beneath the willow tree. She'd sketched, and resketched that image nearly a dozen times until it was right.

"Then, one day," she read on, "the little boy realized there was one thing he loved more than their adventures or story time." Esther's breath caught.

Slowly she turned the page.

"But then the farewells began. First, the boy, who wasn't so little any longer, had to leave. Then, the girl, who was now a beautiful young woman also had to go."

Esther turned to the page representing her time in India while Quintin struggled with his estate. "Their adventures changed. Instead of facing imaginary foe, they both had to confront very real challenges. They had already said farewell to one another; this time they had to say farewell to their comfort, their peace of mind, even to some of their ideals."

Esther took a deep breath. She didn't know what he would have to say about the next part. She'd wondered ever since returning from India if he would understand why she did what she did.

She was about to find out.

The next image was her dancing with Lord Copeland, unable to keep her eyes off Quintin.

"Finally, the day came when the boy and the girl were reunited. But with so many farewells between them, they weren't sure how to say hello."

She turned to the page of him sitting behind her at the musicale. She could clearly remember the mixture of emotions that night; she was elated to see him, overjoyed that he still wanted her, yet terrified of him learning the truth. What a fool she'd been to hide it for so long.

"So they began much as they had the first time," she read. "As friends."

The picture of them among ribbons at Bloomstale's. "As co-conspirators."

Them at Hyde Park. "As the one person the other could always count on."

Esther knew the next picture was of the disaster at the Monstat-tens' home, when Lord Copeland had twisted her words. She summoned all her newfound bravery and turned the page.

"But they weren't what they had been the first time. They weren't children any longer and the foes they faced were far from imaginary."

Esther hurried on to the next page. The one of her explaining the truth to Quintin the morning he'd said he was planning to quit London. "The farewells began to stack up until, it seemed, there was no other option but to say farewell to each other forever."

The next page showed Lily Bay bucking Esther off, while Quintin, in what was clearly another place, returned to his estate books. "The two, now gentleman and lady, continued to fight their foes, but apart this time. Apart, and very sad."

Next was Esther speaking with Lady Helen in the garden. "But then the woman realized something."

Quintin leaned in. "I didn't know the whole of that picture, so I took a few liberties."

Esther glanced up at him. He wasn't smiling as he had before, but the hope in his eyes was all the brighter. "The woman learned that she'd been wrong to say farewell to the man," Esther explained.

She turned the page, showing the image of her creating the book. Quintin's words read, "And she faced this newest foe—the separation between them—in her usual creative and beautiful way."

She lifted a hand to turn the page but couldn't. Those few words struck her forcibly. Esther looked up at him again. "Do you really think I'm creative and beautiful?"

"I think you're that and more."

"Even knowing the horrid thing I did?"

He placed his hand against her cheek. "It doesn't change who you are. You, Esther, are still and always will be all loveliness and grace."

She blinked and a couple of tears made their way down her cheek. "Thank you," she whispered.

"It's not over yet," he said, turning the page to the image of what they were doing now, speaking beneath the willow tree. *Their* willow tree.

Esther blinked a few more times until her eyes cleared enough for her to read. "So, like true friends, true conspirators, they met once more. And there it was decided . . ."

"I took a few *more* liberties on the next page," Quintin said. For the first time, he seemed nervous and he didn't meet her eyes.

Unsure what she would find, Esther turned the page. The top portion was still empty, ready for her to add an image, no doubt. His words filled the bottom.

"They needed to share one last farewell."

Esther's voice caught, but she read on.

"This time, it was not farewell to one another but farewell to their times away from each other. Farwell to their lonely nights and estranged days. Farewell to their fears and their self-doubts. They were not a girl and boy any longer, but a grown woman and man. And so, the man kissed the woman, there beneath their willow tree, and with that kiss they said farewell to being apart ever again. It was the grandest and greatest of farewell kisses ever to be known."

Esther slowly lowered the book, placing it beside the tree trunk and standing straight once more. "The end."

"Not really," Quintin said, his hand opening and closing by his side. "I was hoping it was more the beginning of the next story. That is . . ." He blew out a slow breath and seemed to be willing his hand to stop clenching. "That is, if you'll have me."

Esther slipped her hand into his recently stilled one. "When did you start doing that? Opening and closing your fist that way?"

A smile tugged at the corner of his lips. "After you left for India. I think I did it because I missed watching your hands fidget."

She moved up closer to him. "Perhaps we should let our hands fidget together from now on?"

"I love you, Esther. I always have and I always will. Even though it does sound a bit cliché to say so aloud."

"That happens when you read so many books."

"I guess so," he said, his smile slowly returning.

"I love you too, Quintin." Going up on tiptoe, Esther pressed her lips against his. It was tender, soft. She began to pull back, but Quintin's arm wrapped around her waist and held her to him. The kiss lengthened and she could feel the years they'd spent, wanting each other, waiting for each other, in that single kiss.

Quintin was right, it was the best farewell kiss of all time.

EPILOGUE

*V*enetia Lockhart sat down heavily against the settee. Esther's newest watercolor sat atop the low table. Venetia picked it up and looked it over. It was a lovely depiction of white sheep speckled across a green field. The title across the bottom read: *Other-Worldly Spirits of the Fluffy Variety*.

Venetia laughed softly. She had no idea what the title meant, but no doubt it was a joke between her and Quintin. They had more than Venetia could count. She supposed that came from growing up together.

The pounding in her head grew worse, forcing her to remember it. Slowly Venetia lowered the image back down. No one else was in the small drawing room, so she rubbed the sides of her head, fully admitting to herself how bad her headache had become just since breakfast. No doubt, one of her cursed fevers was upon her.

The door swung open with a bang and Quintin rushed into the room. Venetia quickly sat up straight and plastered on her easiest smile. She wasn't ready to return to her bedchamber yet, so she would hide the onset of her newest fever as long as possible.

Quintin's step slowed the moment he saw her.

Venetia smiled sweetly as he rounded the settee and stared at her, drawing in heavy breathes from his dash down the stairs.

"I don't believe it," he said.

"I told you the servants' halls were a much faster way to get here," she said sweetly, ignoring the pulsing in her brainbox.

He smiled and shook his head. "I wish now I'd have known when we were children."

"It does makes swiping biscuits from the kitchen much easier."

He chuckled. "No doubt."

"Who's been swiping biscuits?" Esther asked, gliding into the room. "Because I want to join them on their next adventure."

Quintin wrapped an arm around his new wife and pulled her close to him. "How about I just ring for a maid to bring us some biscuits now?"

"Where would be the fun in that?" she said, swatting him affectionately.

Venetia smiled and listed her head as she watched them flirt. She never got tired of seeing people in love.

"Then," Quintin continued, his voice dropping lower, "I shall tell the maid to bring in some tea cakes."

"Ooh," Esther sighed. "I do love Cook's tea cakes."

"Done." Quintin kissed her quickly on the cheek and then moved away to ring for a servant.

"Truly, my love," Esther said, sitting next to Venetia, "I'm still amazed at Cook's offerings. I feel positively lucky to have such a woman in our household."

Quintin's smile only grew. "I know."

Heavy footsteps echoed from just outside the drawing room door. "Is it safe to enter?" came the deep voice.

That could only be one person. "You are free to enter, Nigel," Venetia called. "But I'll warn you, both Quintin *and* Esther are present and tea cakes are about to be served."

From the hallway, Nigel groaned. Apparently, Cassandra's husband had unwillingly stumbled upon Quintin and Esther kissing a few days ago and had been quite reluctant to enter any room where they both were residing since.

Cassandra's voice came from the hallway. Though Venetia couldn't make out the exact words, she gathered Cassandra was scolding her husband and shooing him into the room. Venetia didn't understand how Cassandra had grown so fond of a man who was quite against showing emotion; though she suspected he'd grown fond enough of Cassandra in turn that he showed his emotions *for her* when they were alone.

Cassandra entered the room first, shaking her head, her stomach beginning to tell tales of their joy to come. Her large husband, veritably the size of a bear, stalked in after her.

"Venetia, dear, how are you feeling today?" Cassandra asked, sitting in the chair nearest the low-burning fire.

"Quite all right," Venetia lied.

"I told your dear mother that Cottonhold was just the place to speed up your recovery," Esther said.

Her recovery, indeed. Just because a woman drew a fever a few times in the space of a month did not mean she needed to retire to the country like some old horse. She was missing her first Season, for heaven's sake. The joy at Quintin's diversion from earlier faded fully away and the irritation that was her new constant companion came back in full force.

"I don't see why everyone feels they must dote on me so," Venetia said, her tone holding more snap than she'd intended.

Every eye gazed at her intently. Apparently, no one else in the room believed she was being overly babied. Oh, stupid headaches. Stupid fevers. Why could she never avoid them?

"Please don't be angry," Esther said softly, reaching out with a hand and placing it on Venetia's. Her eyes widened and, too late, Venetia pulled away. "Why, you're burning up even now."

Blast. She'd been found out. Now she wouldn't even get some of Cook's delicious tea cakes.

Pulling off a glove, Cassandra stood and moved directly in front of Venetia. She placed her hand against Venetia's forehead.

"It's true. You've another fever."

"It's only a little one," Venetia tried.

"A little one?" Cassandra scoffed. "Off to bed with you this instant. If you grow *worse,* what will Penelope say?"

Venetia slumped. Her mother would say that she couldn't return for the end of the Season, and possibly not even for next year's Season.

"Very well," Venetia said, slowly pushing herself to a stand. The room swam a little as she stood, but Venetia didn't let it show. She'd had much practice hiding such things.

Cassandra turned toward the rest of the room. "I'll just see her settled and—"

"No, that's quite all right," Venetia said, moving through the room and toward the door. "I can see myself to bed easily enough."

"Are you certain?" Esther asked.

"Oh yes," Venetia was sure to keep her tone unaffected this time. "I have done it many times."

Venetia stepped from the drawing room but didn't head for the stairs right away. Instead she moved out of sight and pressed her back against the wall. Apparently, she had a minimum of three days of solitude to look forward to. All she wanted was her Season. All she wanted was to dance past midnight and meet gentlemen and wear fine gowns. She wanted to make friends and catch someone's eye.

She wanted love.

Peeking back around the corner of the open door, Venetia silently spied on her siblings and their spouses. Nigel had taken hold of Cassandra's hand and Quintin had moved to sit beside Esther on the settee, his arm around her shoulders. What would that be like? To care for one person so much it hurt? To have that person respond with affection and consideration?

She closed her eyes. Her lids felt hot; she was feeling all the signs of a troublesome fever.

A small clink made Venetia open her eyes. A young maid with a tray of tea and cakes moved around her toward the drawing room door.

"One minute, if you please," Venetia said softly enough that none of her family would overhear.

The maid paused by the door, clearly confused.

Venetia didn't explain but reached out, snagging one strawberry cake and two lemons. "Now you may go in."

The maid curtsied without spilling anything and continued into the drawing room.

Venetia pushed herself toward the stairs and her bedchamber, slowly chewing on the spongy strawberry cake. All she needed to do now was get well enough that the fevers stayed short and far between. Her best option was to do whatever Mother, or a doctor, recommended. She would get better. She would find ways to heal herself.

And then, next year, she would have a glorious Season; she wanted nothing more.

She took the stairs slowly, the sound of Esther's laugh following after her. Perhaps she could convince Mother and Father to let her stay with Felix and Jocelyn for a time. She always felt better up North where the forests were a bit wild.

Venetia paused as she reached the landing. She could feel herself shaking slightly, but she set her jaw against all opposition. She was determined she would enjoy next year's Season to its fullest extent, and nothing between now and then would distract her from that solitary goal.

The End

THE ROMANCE CONTINUES WITH VENETIA'S STORY IN
A WELL-KEPT PROMISE

He's been waiting months for her to finally notice him.
Except suddenly, he's not the only one vying for her hand.

Download the short story for free at:
www.LauraRollins.com

ACKNOWLEDGMENTS

No book is ever written without much encouragement and support from any number of people. I am forever thankful to my husband and children, as their patience and love is the reason I get to do this.

Special thanks go to my writing groups, for their advice and help. Also to Jenny Proctor and Emily Poole; without your suggestions and edits this book would not have been half so good.

Lastly, thanks to my Father in Heaven, for giving me a beautiful life and the opportunity to create.

ABOUT THE AUTHOR

Laura Rollins has always loved a heart-melting happily ever after. It didn't matter if the story took place in Regency England, in outer space, beneath the Earth's crust, or in a cobbler's shop, if there was a sweet romance, she would read it.

Life has given her many of her own adventures. Currently she lives in the Rocky Mountains with her best-friend, who is also her husband, and their four beautiful children. She still loves to read books and more books; her favorite types of music are classical, Broadway, and country; she'd rather be hiking the mountains than twiddling her thumbs on the beach; and she's been known to debate with her oldest son over whether Infinity is better categorized as a number or an idea.

You can learn more about her and her books, as well as pick up a free story, at:

www.LauraRollins.com

Printed in Great Britain
by Amazon